I
AM
WATCHING
YOU

ALSO BY TERESA DRISCOLL

Recipes for Melissa
Last Kiss Goodnight

I
AM
WATCHING
YOU

TERESA DRISCOLL

THOMAS & MERCER

Text copyright © 2017 Teresa Driscoll
All rights reserved.

Published by Thomas & Mercer, Seattle

www.apub.com

Amazon, the Amazon logo, and Thomas & Mercer are trademarks of Amazon.com, Inc., or its affiliates.

ISBN-13: 9781542046596
ISBN-10: 1542046599

Cover design by Tom Sanderson

Printed in the United States of America

I
AM
WATCHING
YOU

JULY 2015

CHAPTER 1

THE WITNESS

I made a mistake. I know that now.

The only reason I did what I did was what I heard on that train. And I ask you, in all truthfulness – how would you have felt?

Until that moment, I had never considered myself prudish. Or naive. OK, OK, so I had a pretty conventional – some might say sheltered – upbringing but . . . Heavens. Look at me now. I've lived a bit. Learned a lot. Pretty average, I would argue, on the Richter scale of moral behaviour, which is why what I heard so shook me.

I thought they were nice girls, you see.

Of course, I really shouldn't listen in on other people's conversations. But it's impossible not to on public transport, don't you find? So many barking into their mobile phones while everyone else ramps up the volume to compete. To be heard.

On reflection, I would probably not have become so sucked in had my book been better, but to my eternal regret I bought the book for the same reason I bought the magazine with wind turbines on the cover.

I read somewhere that by your forties you are supposed to care more about what you think of others than what they think of you – so why is it I am still waiting for this to kick in?

If you want to buy Hello! *magazine, just buy it, Ella.* What does it matter what the bored student on the cash desk thinks?

But no. I pick the obscure environmental magazine and the worthy biography, so that by the time the two young men get on with their black plastic bin bags at Exeter, I am bored to my very bones.

A question for you now.

What would you think if you saw two men board a train, each holding a black bin bag – contents unknown? For myself, the mother of a teenage son whose bedroom is subject to a health and safety order, I merely think, *Typical. Couldn't even find a holdall, lads?*

They are loud and boisterous, skylarking in the way that so many men in their twenties do – only just making the train, with the plumped-up platform guard blowing his whistle in furious disapproval.

After messing about with the automatic door – *open, shut, open, shut* – which they inevitably find hilarious beyond the facts, they settle into the seats nearest the luggage racks. But then, apparently spotting the two girls from Cornwall, they glance knowingly at each other and head further down the carriage to the seats directly behind them.

I smile to myself. See, I'm no killjoy. I was young once.

I watch the girls go all quiet and shy, one widening her eyes at her friend – and yes, one of the men is especially striking, like a model or a member of a boy band. And it all reminds me of that very particular feeling in your tummy.

You know.

So I am not at all surprised or in the least bit disapproving when the men stand up and the good-looking one then leans over the top of the dividing seats, wondering if he might fetch the girls something from the buffet, '. . . seeing as I'm going?'

Next there are name swaps and quite a bit of giggling, and the dance begins.

Two coffees and four lagers later, the young men have joined the girls – all seated near enough for me to follow the full conversation.

I know, I know. I really shouldn't be listening, but we've been over this. I'm bored, remember. They're loud.

So then. The girls repeat what I have already gleaned from their earlier gossiping. This trip to London is their first solo visit to the capital – a gift from their parents to celebrate the end of GCSEs. They are booked into a budget hotel, have tickets for *Les Misérables* and have never been this excited.

'You kidding me? You really never been to London on your own before?' Karl, the boy-band lookalike, is amazed. 'Can be a tricky place, you know, girls. London. You need to watch yourselves. Taxi not tube when you get out of the theatre. You hear me?'

I am liking Karl now. He is recommending shops and market stalls – also a club where he says they will be safe if they fancy some decent music and dancing after the show. He is writing down the name on a piece of paper for them. Knows the bouncer. 'Mention my name, OK?'

And then Anna, the taller of the two friends from Cornwall, is wondering about the black bags and I am secretly delighted that she has asked, for I am curious also, smiling in anticipation of the teasing. *Boys. So disorganised. What are you like, eh?*

But no.

The two young men have just got out of prison. The black bags contain their personal effects.

I can actually hear myself swallowing then – a rush of fluid suddenly filling the back of my throat and my pulse now unwelcome percussion in my ear.

The pause button is pressed, but not for long enough. Much too quickly, the girls are regrouping. 'You having us on?'

5

No. The boys are not having them on. They have decided to be straight with people. Have made their mistakes and paid their dues but refuse to be ashamed.

Cards on the table, girls? Karl has served a sentence at Exeter prison for assault; Antony for theft. Karl was merely sticking up for a friend, you understand, and – hand on heart – would do the same again. His friend was being picked on in a bar and he hates bullying.

Me, I am struggling with the paradox – bullying versus assault, and do we really lock people up for minor altercations? – but the girls seem fascinated, and in their sweet and liberal naivety are saying that loyalty is a good thing and they had a bloke from prison who came into their school once and told them how he had completely turned his life around after serving time over drugs. Covered in tattoos, he was. *Covered.*

'Wow. Jail. So what was that really like?'

It is at this point I consider my role.

Privately I am picturing Anna's mother toasting her bottom by her Aga, worrying with her husband if their little girl will be all right, and he is telling her not to fuss so. *They are growing up fast. Sensible girls. They will be fine, love.*

And I am thinking that they are not fine at all. For Karl is now thinking that the safest thing for the girls would be to have someone who knows London well chaperoning them during their visit.

Karl and Antony are going to stay with friends in Vauxhall and fancy a big night to celebrate their release. How about they meet the girls after the theatre and try the club together?

This is when I decide that I need to phone the girls' parents. They have named their hamlet. Anna lives on a farm. It's not rocket science. I can phone the post office or local pub; how many farms can there be?

But now Anna isn't sure at all. No. They should probably have an early night so they can hit the shops tomorrow morning. They have this plan, see, to go to Liberty's first thing because Sarah is determined to try on something by Stella McCartney and get a picture on her phone.

Good girl, I am thinking. Sensible girl. *Spare me the intervention, Anna.* But there is a complication, for Sarah seems suddenly to have taken a shine to Antony. There is a second trip to the buffet and they swap seats on their return – Anna now sitting with Karl and Sarah with Antony, who is telling her about his regrets at stuffing up his life. He only turned to crime out of desperation, he says, because he couldn't get a job. Couldn't support his son.

Son?

It sweeps over me, then. The shadow from the thatched canopy of my chocolate-box life – me shrinking smaller and smaller into the shade as Antony explains that he is fighting his ex for access, telling Sarah that there is no way he is going to have his son growing up not knowing his dad. 'Don't you think that would be just terrible, Sarah? For him to grow up not knowing his dad?'

Sarah is the one who is surprising me now – there's a catch in her throat as she says she thinks it's really cool that he cares so very much, because many young men wouldn't, would just walk away from the responsibility. 'I feel really awful now. Us banging on about Stella McCartney.'

And the truth? At this point I have absolutely no idea about any of it anymore. What do I know? A woman whose son's only access battle involved an 18-certificate film at the local cinema.

An hour of whispering follows and I try very hard to read again, to take in the pluses of the quieter generation of wind turbines, but then Antony and Sarah are off to the buffet again. *More lager*, I am thinking. *Big mistake, Sarah.* And this is when I decide.

Yes. I will head to the buffet myself on the pretext of needing coffee, and in the queue or passing in the corridor will feign trouble with my phone. I will ask Sarah for help – hoping to separate her from Antony for a quiet word – and give a little warning that she needs to step away from this nonsense or I will be phoning her parents. *Immediately, you understand me, Sarah? I can find out their number.*

Our carriage is three away from the buffet. I stumble into seats passing through the second, bump-bump-bumping my thighs, and then feel for my phone in the pocket of my jacket as I pass through the automatic doors into the connecting space.

And that's when I hear them.

No shame. No attempt even to keep themselves quiet about it. Making out, loud and proud, in the train toilet. Rutting in the cubicle like a pair of animals.

I know it's them from what he's saying. How long it's been. How grateful he is. 'Sarah, oh Sarah . . .'

And yes, I admit it. I am completely shocked to the core of my very being. Hot with humiliation. Furious. Winded and desperate, more than anything on this planet, to escape the noise.

Also the shame of my naivety. My ridiculous assumptions.

I stumble across the corridor to the next set of automatic doors and into the carriage, breathless and flustered in the scramble to put distance between myself and the evidence of my miscalculation.

Nice girls?

In the buffet queue, I am listening again to the pulse in my ear as I wonder if someone else will have heard them by now. Even reported them?

And then I am thinking, *Report them? Report them to whom, Ella? Will you just listen to yourself? Other people will do precisely what you should have done from the off. They will mind their own.*

At which point my emotions begin to change and I am wondering instead how I came to be this out of touch, this buttoned up. This woman who evidently has not the first clue about young people. Or anything much.

Into my head now – a kaleidoscope of memories. Pictures torn around the edges. The magazines we found in our son's room. That night after the cinema when we came home early to find Luke trying to override the Sky security to watch porn.

So that on this wretched train, I find that I need very urgently to speak to my husband. To my Tony. To reset my compass.

I need to ask him if the whole problem here is not with them but with me. *Am I altogether ridiculous, Tony? No, really – I need you to be honest with me. When we had that row over the Sky channels and Luke's magazines.*

Am I the most terrible prude? Am I?

I do try to ring him, actually – that night from the hotel after the conference session. I want to tell him how I did the sensible thing and moved to the other end of the train. Minded my own. The girls clearly quite streetwise enough.

But he is out and hasn't taken his mobile, being one of the few who still thinks they give you brain cancer, and so I speak instead to Luke and find that it calms me to hear him describe supper – a tagine from a recipe he downloaded on a new app. He loves to cook, my Luke, and I am teasing him about the state of the kitchen, betting he has used every appliance and pan on the property.

Then it is the morning in the hotel.

I so hate this sensation – that out-of-body numbness born of air conditioning, a foreign bed and lack of discipline over the minibar. My hotel treat – a brandy or two after a long day.

It is barely six thirty and I long for more sleep. Ten futile minutes and I give up, eyeing the sachets of sadness in the little bowl alongside the kettle. I always do this in hotel rooms. Kid myself that I will drink instant coffee just this once, only to pour it down the bathroom sink.

I stare at the line of empty miniatures, wincing as a terrible thought flutters into the room. I glance at the phone by the bed and feel a punch of dread, the familiar frisson of fear that I have done something embarrassing, something I am going to regret.

I turn back to the row of bottles and remember that after the second brandy last night, I decided to phone directory enquiries to track down the girls' parents. I go cold momentarily at the thought of this, my memory still hazy. *Did you actually ring? Think, Ella, think.*

I stare again at the phone and concentrate hard. Ah, yes. I am remembering now, my shoulders relaxing as I finally see it. I was holding the phone and then at the *very* point of dialling, I realised that I wasn't thinking straight, and not just because of the brandy. My motivation was skewed. I wanted to phone not because I was worried for the girls, but as a punishment, because I was angry at how Sarah had made me feel.

And so I did the sensible thing. I put the phone back down, I turned out the light and I went to sleep.

Good. This is very good. The relief now so overwhelming that I decide by way of celebration that I will try the instant coffee after all.

I flick on the kettle first and then the television. And that is when it comes. The single moment – suspended at first and then stretching, stretching, beyond this room, beyond this city. The moment in time in which I realise my life is never going to be the same again.

Not ever.

The sound is muted from the late-night film I watched with the subtitles on to spare disturbing the guests next door.

But the picture is unmistakable. Beautiful. A photograph from her Facebook page. Her green eyes glowing and her blonde hair cascading down her back. She is at the beach; I recognise St Michael's Mount behind her.

And somehow my body has zoomed backwards – through the pillow and the bedstead and the wall – until I am watching the screen from much further away. This screen that is scrolling putrid, awful words: *Missing . . . Anna . . . Missing . . . Anna . . .* The kettle screaming angry clouds onto the mirror while I am planning the calls in my head all at once.

A black and terrible jumble of excuses. None of them good enough. To the police. To Tony.

You have to understand that I was going to phone . . .

CHAPTER 2

THE FATHER

Henry Ballard sits in the conservatory, trying very hard to ignore the clattering in the kitchen.

He knows that he should go to his wife – to help her, to console her – but he knows also that it will make no difference and so is putting it off. The truth? He wants just a little longer like this, looking out on the lawn. In this strange space, this addition to the house that has never really worked – always too hot or too cold, despite all the blinds and the big dust-magnet fan they had installed at ridiculous expense – he has managed somehow to drift into a state of semi-consciousness, a place in which his mind can roam beyond his body, beyond time, out into the garden where this very minute, in the early morning light, he is listening to them whispering in their den in the bushes. Anna and Jenny.

It was their favourite place for a year, maybe two, when they were into that hideous pink phase. Pink duvets. Pink Barbies. Pink tent bought from some catalogue and filled with all manner of girly paraphernalia. He had always refused to go near the thing. Now he wanted more than anything in the world to forget the milking and the hay, the VAT forms and the bank, and to float out there and make a little fire to cook sausages for their breakfast. Proper camping, like he promised to do so many times, but never did.

Now an almighty crash from the kitchen brings him back inside. She is picking up tins from the floor – a collection of bun and baking cases in all manner of sizes and shapes.

'What on earth are you doing?'

'Plum slices.'

'Oh, for Christ's sake, Barbara.'

Anna's favourite. A sort of flapjack with spiced stewed plums through the middle. He can smell the cinnamon: the spice jar is tipped over on the kitchen surface, the pungent spill a neat tiny hill.

Oh, Barbara.

He watches her picking up all the tins, her hands trembling, and simply cannot bear it.

And so, instead of helping and trying to be in any way kind or even decent, he goes into his study and sits by the phone so that five, maybe ten minutes later, he is the first to see the police car pull up again on the drive outside.

Something terrible wrenches in his stomach then, and he actually thinks for a moment of barricading the door – a ridiculous image of all the hallway furniture piled up high so that they cannot come in. There are two of them this time. A man and a woman. The man in a suit and the woman in uniform.

By the time he is in the hall, his wife is standing in the kitchen doorway in her apron, wiping her hands dry over and over and over. He turns to look at her for just a moment, and her eyes plead with him and with God and with justice.

He opens the door – Anna and Jenny rushing in with their school bags and tennis rackets, chucking them all onto the floor. Relief. Relief. Relief.

Then for real.

Their faces say it.

'Have you found her?'

The man in his creased high-street suit just shakes his head.

'This is the family liaison officer. PC Cathy Bright. We talked about her on the phone?'

He can say nothing. Mute.

'Is it all right if we come in, Mr Ballard?'

A nod. All he can muster.

In the study they all sit and there is a strange shushing noise, flesh on flesh, as his wife rubs her palms together, and so he reaches out to take her hand. To stop the noise.

'As we said before, the police in London – the Metropolitan team – they are doing everything they can. They've fast-tracked the case, given Anna's age. The circumstances. They are in contact with us constantly.'

'I want to go to London. To help—'

'Mr Ballard. We discussed this. Your wife needs you here and there are things we need help with here, too. It is better for now, please, if we can concentrate on gathering all the information that we need. If there is any news – anything at all – I promise you that you will be told and we will arrange transport immediately.'

'So has Sarah remembered anything? Said anything more? We would like to speak to her. If we could just speak to her.'

'Sarah is still in shock. It's understandable. There is a specialist team on hand and her parents are with her now. We are all trying to get what information we can. Officers in London are going over all the CCTV footage. From the club.'

'I still don't get it. Club? What were they doing in a club? There was nothing in the plan about any club. They had tickets for *Les Misérables*. We expressly said that—'

'And there is a new development which may throw some light on that, Mr Ballard.'

The sound his throat makes as he tries to clear it seems too loud. Guttural. Gross.

'A witness has come forward. Someone who was on the train.'

Phlegm. In his throat.

'Witness. What do you mean, *witness*? Witness to what? I'm not understanding.'

The two police officers exchange a look, and the woman moves to the chair next to Barbara.

The detective does the talking. 'A woman who was sitting near Anna and Sarah on the journey has phoned in after the police appeal. She says she overheard the two girls striking up an acquaintance with two men on the train.'

'What do you mean, *acquaintance*? What men? I'm not following you.' His wife is now gripping his hand more tightly.

'From what she heard, Mr and Mrs Ballard, it appears that Anna and Sarah may have become friendly with two men. Who are *known* to us.'

'Men? What men?'

'Men who had just got out of prison, Mr Ballard.'

'No. No. She must be mistaken . . . There's no way. Absolutely no way.'

'The police in London are going to try to speak to Sarah some more about this. Urgently. And to this witness. As I say, we just need to piece together as much detail as we can about what happened before Anna went missing.'

'It's been hours and hours.'

'Yes.'

'They're sensible girls, officer. You understand that? Good, sensible girls. Brought up right. We would never – never – have let them go on the trip if we didn't—'

'Yes. Yes. Of course. And you must try very hard to stay positive. Like I say. We are doing everything we possibly can to find Anna, and we will keep you informed every step of the way. Cathy can stay with you. Answer any questions you may have. I'd just like to have another look at Anna's room, if I may. We are hoping there may be a diary. Have a look at her computer. That sort of thing. Could you show me, Mr Ballard? While Cathy perhaps makes a cup of tea for your wife. Yes?'

He isn't listening now. He is thinking that she didn't want them to go. His wife. She said they were too young. It was too far. Too soon. He was the one who spoke up for the trip. *Oh, for heaven's sake, Barbara. You can't baby them forever.* The truth? He felt Anna needed to step away from the apron strings.

Away from the plum slices.

But it wasn't only that. Dear God.

What if they found out that it *wasn't only that*?

CHAPTER 3

THE FRIEND

In a stuffy twin room of the inappropriately named Paradise Hotel in London, Sarah can hear her mother's voice whispering her name and so keeps her eyes resolutely shut.

It is a different room now. Identical but on a different floor. The one in which she unpacked with Anna remains off limits, though Sarah cannot understand why. Anna did not go back there. Did they not believe her? *She did not come back here. OK?*

In this room there is still a horrid, ill-defined smell. Something that reminds her of the back of a cupboard. Hide-and-seek as a child. With her eyes closed, Sarah wishes she could play the game right now. Ignore the smell and the temperature, her mother and the police, and play hide-and-seek. Yes. The time-slip version in which Anna is drying her hair around now – the tongs already hot for straightening afterwards – blabbing on above the drone of the motor about what they should do today. Which shop should they visit first? And was Sarah serious about trying on the Stella McCartney range because the assistant would be able to tell from their clothes that they weren't actually going to buy anything.

Anna. Sweet, infuriating Anna. Too skinny. Too beautiful. Too—

'Are you awake, love? Can you hear me, darling?'

Sarah, facing away from her mother still, opens her eyes and winces at the light fighting through the chink in the curtains to shape a triangle on the wall. She had lain on the bed fully clothed, refusing to get under the covers, so sure there would be news by now. Any minute. They would find her any minute.

'I'm glad you managed to drop off, love. Even just an hour. I've made us some tea.'

'I don't want anything.'

'Just a sip. Two sugars. You need to get something inside you. Some sugar—'

'I said I can't face it. All right?'

Her mother is in the same trousers as yesterday but a fresh blouse now, and Sarah is thinking it is both typical and somehow inappropriate that she thought to bring a clean blouse.

'Your father's arrived. He's downstairs. He's been with the police mostly. They want to speak to you again. When you feel—'

'I've told them everything I can remember already. Hours of it. And I don't want to see my father. You shouldn't have called him.'

Sarah and her mother lock eyes.

'Look, I know it's difficult, darling. You and your dad. But the thing is, he does care. And they've had some call, the police, that they want to talk to you about. After the coverage on the telly.'

'Call?'

'Yes. From some woman on the train.'

'Woman? I don't know what you're talking about. What woman?'

Sarah can feel the same gaping hole in her stomach that she felt in those first terrible hours, while she waited with the police for her mother. While she was still woozy from the booze. Disorientated. *Where are you, Anna? Where the hell are you?*

Trying to give the officers just enough detail to make them take it all seriously but not enough to—

She gets up quickly now, feeling the crumple of her linen shirt against her waist as she moves, fussing with the hairbrushes, make-up bags and other junk on the dressing table.

'Have you got the remote? I need to see the news. What they're saying. What *are* they saying?'

'I don't think that's a good idea, Sarah. Drink your tea. I'll tell your dad you're awake. That they can come up now.'

'I'm not speaking to them again. Not yet.'

'Look, darling. I realise this is awful. For you. For all of us.' Her mother is moving across the room now. 'But they'll find her, love. I'm sure they will. She probably went off to some party and is afraid she's in trouble.' She puts her arm around Sarah's shoulders – the mugs of tea now positioned amid the chaos of the dressing table – but Sarah shrugs her off.

'Are Anna's parents here?'

'Not yet. I don't know. I don't know what's been decided about that. The police wanted to check some things with them in Cornwall.'

'What things?'

'Computers or something. I don't know. I don't exactly remember, Sarah. It's all been a blur. They just want to get all the information they can to help with this. With the search.'

'And you think I don't? You think I don't feel bad enough?'

'No one's blaming you, love.'

'Blaming me? So why say *blaming me* if no one's blaming me?'

'Sarah . . . love. Don't be like this. They're going to find her. I know they are. I'll ring downstairs.'

'No. I need you to leave me alone. All of you. I need you to just leave me alone now.'

Sarah's mother takes her mobile from her pocket and is just feeling around for her glasses when there is a tap at the door.

'That'll probably be them now.'

It is the same detective as before, but with a different woman police officer this time and Sarah's father alongside.

'So, is there any news?' Sarah's mother begins to raise her body from the chair but slumps back down as their heads shake a 'no' in stereo.

'Did you manage to rest, Sarah? Feel OK to talk some more now?' It is the woman police officer.

'I wasn't drunk. When we spoke before. I wasn't drunk.'

'No.'

The adults all look from one to the other.

'We've had a look at the CCTV, Sarah. From the club.' It is the detective's voice now – firmer. 'Some of the cameras weren't working, unfortunately. But there are some things we're not quite understanding, Sarah. Also, we've had a call from a witness.'

'A witness?'

'Yes. A woman on the train.'

She feels it instantly. The frisson. The giveaway. The cooling as the blood shifts.

Draining from her face.

ONE YEAR ON

July 2016

CHAPTER 4

THE WITNESS

I never deluded myself.

I always knew what this week would be like. One part of me longing for it: the slim hope the anniversary coverage might kick-start things again for the investigation. But the other part: pure dread. People giving me that look again. *That woman. Do you remember? The woman who didn't say anything. On the train. Do you remember? When that girl disappeared? Christ – is it a year ago already?*

But I do still want it – the reconstruction on *Crimecatchers*, for the family. That poor mother. I just don't want to be a part of it.

You can understand that, can't you? I mean, I didn't mind them asking. Although Tony went ballistic when the police phoned up – surprised they had the gall.

You leak her name. You let everyone judge her and you think she wants to be on your television programme . . .

He still insists it was a deliberate leak – the press getting my name. We have no proof and I have got to the point, to be frank, where I am not sure I care one way or the other; all I know is that I cannot bear the thought of everyone turning up all over again. Raking it up all over again. Judging me. Hating me.

Even loyal customers in the shop giving me that slightly odd look. Deliberately not mentioning it.

The official version from the police press office is that there was no leak; they merely mentioned to a few reporters that the witness on the train was 'attending a conference'. But they must have said what kind of conference, otherwise how did the press know I was a florist? Whatever. Some of the press pack checked out the various floristry events, worked through the lists of delegates from Devon and Cornwall, and eventually landed at our door.

I still go cold, thinking about it.

Of course, if I'd been smarter they would have had no way of confirming it. If I had thought to say, *I don't know what you're talking about,* they would have had to leave it at that. But I didn't.

I know this is going to sound completely stupid but what I said in my complete disorientation on the doorstep was, *Who gave you my name?*

Why the hell did you say that? was the first thing Tony asked. *Jesus, Ella. You gave it to them on a plate.*

But I didn't; not really. I didn't let any of the reporters in. I didn't give them any quotes, I swear, but they still took my picture, and they phoned and phoned and phoned until we had to change the number.

'Harassment', Tony called it. *Hasn't she been through enough?* Bless him. My sweet, sweet man.

And then things turned really nasty. Horrid stuff on social media. Until in the end we had to close down the shop for a bit.

But here's the thing. As horrid as it all was, I still don't think I have been through enough. She's still gone – that beautiful girl. Most probably dead – almost certainly dead – although from what I hear, her poor mother still clings to the hope that she's alive.

And can you blame her? I probably would, too.

The police liaison officer for *Crimecatchers* told me that Mrs Ballard has given a really harrowing interview. I'm not even sure I can watch. Anna's mother has spent the last year collecting all this information on missing girls who have eventually turned up years later. You know – held captive by some loon, brainwashed and then finally escaped. They had to cut all that out of the interview, apparently, as it's not the police's focus at all. They obviously think Anna is most probably dead. This is about finding a killer, not finding a loon with a girl in his basement.

Out of sensitivity, they have kept all of Mrs Ballard's stories about Anna as a little girl. All her hopes and her dreams. That's apparently just the sort of thing that makes people phone in with new information. But it's all about finding the two men. Finding the body, I suppose. Makes me go cold to think of that . . .

And this is where Tony gets really angry. His take is if the police hadn't been so slow in putting out the appeal to trace Karl and Antony after I tipped them off, then maybe they would have stopped them doing a bunk. Most probably abroad.

As far as I can tell, the delay was something to do with Sarah. The police are diplomatic but, putting two and two together, it seems at first she denied ever meeting them. The men on the train. Said I was a fantasist. It was only when they went over all the CCTV footage and finally found a couple of shots of them getting off the train together, and also outside the station, that the police even put their pictures out. Too late.

But that, of course, is where it all goes wrong and it all comes back to me.

If I had phoned in a warning in the first place. If I had stepped up. Stepped in.

You are not to think like that. You can't take the world on your shoulders. You did nothing wrong. Nothing, Ella. It was those men. Not you. You can't go on blaming yourself.

25

Can't I, Tony?

And I'm not the only one now.

The first postcard came a few days ago.

At first I was so shaken when I read it, I had to go straight to the bathroom. Vomited.

I can't explain why I felt so very scared. Shock, I suppose, because initially it seemed so threatening, so darned nasty. And then when I finally calmed down and thought it all through, I suddenly realised who'd sent it. And with that came a mixture of relief and crippling guilt. To be perfectly honest with you, I probably deserve it.

It was just anger. Not a real threat; just lashing out.

That first postcard was inside an envelope. A black card with letters cut out of a magazine. WHY DIDN'T YOU HELP HER? It was just like you see on a television drama, and not even very well done. Still sticky to the touch.

I was stupid; I ripped it up and put it in the bin because I didn't want Tony to see. I knew he would phone the police and I didn't want that. Them round here. The press round here. All that craziness all over again.

It took me a while to process it properly. To start with, I thought it was just another random nutter, but then I thought, *Hang on a minute, the anniversary appeal hasn't even been on the telly yet.*

The truth is the story has been forgotten. Until the programme tonight, no one else will have given it a second thought. That's how it works – why it's so difficult for the police. It's all people talk about one minute, and then the next, everyone forgets.

Then today another card arrived. Black again, with a nastier message. BITCH . . . HOW DO YOU SLEEP?

So that I see it even more clearly now. This *is* my fault. This is to pay me back, not just for what I didn't do for Anna, but for going down there in the summer.

I know exactly who the postcards are from now . . .

CHAPTER 5

THE FATHER

Henry Ballard checks his watch and whistles for Sammy.

In the distance, he can see smoke just emerging from one of the holiday lets – a former barn that was once his father's destination at this same time of an evening. The final check of the livestock before supper.

Henry still takes the same stroll each night himself, but with a quiet sorrow now.

Anna's voice haunting him as he walks.

You disgust me, Dad . . .

Henry closes his eyes and waits for the voice to quieten. By the time he opens his eyes there is a stronger curl of smoke from the chimney ahead.

It all made *economic sense*, of course. The conversions. It became Barbara's favourite phrase, and the bank's, too. *Makes good economic sense, Henry.*

The agricultural success story that was Ladbrook Farm had been four generations in the making. It survived the rise and fall of local mining. It survived the changing tastes of the consumer market. It won rosettes for rare breeds. It even branched out into daffodils at one point. But the segue from full working farm to what his colleagues now dismiss as *Still playing at it, H?* took but a blink.

Tourism is the business he is in now, not farming. And yes – it makes absolute sense financially. One set of barns was converted and sold to pay off all the outstanding loans more than a decade back. A second set is now rental properties, and that is more than enough income on top of the teashop and campsite – and certainly more regular profit than his father or his grandfather had dared hope for.

The truth? They put in the slog, his ancestors. They paid off the bulk of the debts to the banks with blood, sweat and tears, too. And him? What has he done?

He has reaped the rewards. There isn't an evening that Henry Ballard has not felt wretched about that.

So yes – he is still playing at it. Messing about on the fringe with his sheep – barely worth the feed – and his tiny rare-breed beef herd.

He has taken this same walk with a heavy heart for years. And now, since Anna?

Henry winces again at the memory of his daughter beside him in the car.

You disgust me . . .

'So what's left now?' he says out loud as Sammy nuzzles his hand, amber eyes turned up to check his master's. The dog still sits under Anna's chair every night during supper. Unbearable.

Henry pats Sammy's head, then sets off for the farmhouse. He is dreading the evening ahead but has promised Barbara they will watch the anniversary appeal together, so he must not be late. They have talked at length about how to handle this, worrying about what is best for Jenny, who has perhaps coped the worst of all. The sister without a sister.

Only eighteen months between the girls – so sweet and so close, especially when they were little. Oh sure, there were fights, too, the usual sibling rivalry, but they were always friends by bedtime, often choosing to share a room, even though there were bedrooms to spare. Henry thinks for a moment of how he used to peek through their door to check on them last thing at night, all arms and legs and pink pyjamas, curled up in a double bed.

That punch to his gut again. Jenny is still not sleeping. Barbara is still not sleeping. He has no idea how they are all supposed to manage it, this TV appeal. The glare of the spotlight all over again.

An invitation to the studios in London was declined as out of the question. Barbara would never have coped with a live interview. No. Henry put his foot down, not least because time around the police made him so very nervous. So all the filming had been done in advance at the house. They had dug out an old video, too, from when Anna was tiny.

He pauses, clenching his fist at the memory of the camera in his hand; Barbara calling directions in the background. A gaggle of friends round for a birthday treat, all of them in fancy dress – cowboys and fairy costumes. A huge chocolate cake with candles. *Get some shots of her blowing out the candles, Henry. Make sure you don't miss a shot of the candles . . .* He thinks of that other version of his wife – Barbara beaming and bustling, at her happiest when the house was full of children and noise and chaos.

Henry clears his throat and leans down to stroke Sammy's head again, feeling the familiar wave of connection. Man to dog. Man and dog to land.

So – yes. They agreed to release some of the birthday video, as the police said moving pictures tended to bring in more calls, which was, of course, the whole point. This first anniversary was a key opportunity, they were told, to resurrect interest in the case. To bring in new leads. To try to find the men from the train. But he and Barbara worry very much about the strain on Jenny. She is also in the clip chosen by the TV producers, smiling alongside her sister, and Barbara and Henry had sat down and made it absolutely clear that if Jenny were even the tiniest bit uncomfortable, they could say no and come up with something else, or ask if her image could be blanked out in some way. But what had broken Henry was how their elder daughter reacted.

It was as if she suddenly saw this light go on, a window of opportunity in the wretched grind of guilt and helplessness. Suddenly her eyes were shining and she was saying that of course she didn't mind people seeing her in a fairy costume with wings. *Dear God. If it might help them find Anna.*

And then she was off to her room, shouting that he was to follow her. There were loads of old pictures in boxes in one of the cupboards. She would dig them out. And could he call the police? *Right now, Daddy.* Loads of really great pictures. *Do you remember? When we used to fool about in those automatic booths. The gang. Me, Sarah and Anna and Paul and Tim.* She found an example – the five of them pulling faces – and held it out to him.

Henry sucks in the cold air as he remembers Anna in the centre of her friends, and closes his eyes.

You disgust me . . .

He had guessed the police wouldn't want the pictures. And they didn't. They just wanted the film. And when he told poor Jenny that the police were very grateful – and he and Mummy were, too – for all the time she had put in, finding the other pictures, her eyes had changed right back to how they always looked now. Sort of only half there.

'Come on then, Sammy. Time to do this.'

Taking his wellies off in the boot room, Henry can hear his wife calling up the stairs.

'Now are you sure you won't watch it with us, Jen? Down here? Daddy and I really don't like the idea – Oh. Hang on. I can hear – Daddy's back.'

He walks in his socks through to the kitchen.

'Great. Good. Henry. I've set it ready on the right channel and it's all set to record, too. The producer has been on from the studio and they're going to ring us. To let us know about the number of calls.'

'Good. That's good.'

'Jennifer is still saying that she wants to watch it in her room. I don't feel at all happy about that, Henry. Will you try talking to her again?'

'If you like. But I spoke to her this morning, love, and—'

'The thing is she doesn't have to watch it at all, if she doesn't want to. I've told her that. But if she does, I don't want her to be on her own. I don't see why she won't be with us. We should be together for this. Don't you think we should be together? As a family. Watch it together.'

Henry wonders if he should say it. The obvious: that they are no longer a family. He examines his wife's face very closely and lowers his voice to a whisper. 'Jenny doesn't want to have to see our faces, darling.' He means hers. Barbara's.

'Our faces?' Barbara's expression changes as she turns the words over for a moment. She looks away to the mirror in the hall and then quickly back at him. 'Is that what she said?'

'She didn't have to, love.'

Henry continues to watch his wife very, very closely as she processes this properly. He makes himself look at her, right in the eye. He knows exactly why it is so difficult for Jenny to do this because he finds it so very difficult these days himself. To witness the depth of it all, written there, dark and dreadful at the very back of Barbara's eyes. All day. Every day. No matter how hard she tries to dress it all up for Jenny with hope and smiles. With her scrapbook cuttings of the lost and found. And her endless baking.

'But you'll still talk to her? Before the programme?' She is looking down at the floor now.

Henry steps forward and kisses his wife on the forehead. It is a kiss of duty and he does not touch her at the same time, for he knows the rules. Their limits. Their physical life on hold; or maybe gone forever.

'I'll just wash my hands and then – yes. I'll talk to her.'

Jenny is sitting on the floor of her room, surrounded by bits of paper. Magazines also, and old photo albums, too.

'Mummy wanted me to have another word.' Henry scans the albums. Lots more photographs of the two sisters growing up. Matching bridesmaid dresses in one. Their first day at big school together. Most of the recent pictures are stored digitally, of course, but Jenny printed off a lot of favourites after her laptop crashed one year and she lost the pictures from a whole summer. They'd already been wiped from the camera. Irretrievable.

'It's all right. I've asked Paul and Sarah and Tim to come over. Is that OK? I mean – Mum's right. It might feel too upsetting to watch it on my own. But I can't sit with Mummy. I just can't.'

'Oh. Right. I'd better have a word. Goodness.' He checks his watch. 'It's just that your mother might not feel comfortable with so many other people in the house this evening.'

'Oh, come on, Dad. These aren't *other people*. They're my friends.'

Henry presses his lips together. There is still an hour and a half until the programme is due to start. He takes a deep breath, trying to weigh up his own response before dealing with his wife's.

Barbara will cater. Sandwiches and cakes and the like. Fussing.

Absent-mindedly he looks at his watch again. Who knows – maybe it will actually help Barbara to have something to fuss over. A distraction.

He is surprised that Sarah's mother Margaret does not want her at home to protect her. It has been hard for Sarah. A lot of unanswered questions. Still no one quite understands the story of how the friends became separated in London, and some people have been pointing fingers.

Privately, Henry is not entirely disapproving. Better for people to be focusing on Sarah . . .

Downstairs, Barbara loads the last of the dishes into the dishwasher as he explains the new turn of events.

'Oh right. I see . . .'

'So – what do you think? Are you OK with this? With a houseful, I mean. I realise Jenny should have discussed this with us first but I didn't like to criticise. Not today.'

Barbara wipes her hands on her apron and undoes the bow at the back.

'I'm not sure it's a good idea, Henry. That's my gut instinct. I mean, I know how close they all are – *were*.' She draws herself up, sucking in a breath.

Henry waits and they let the moment hang between them. No one knows what tense to use.

'But everyone's been so on edge lately.' She is lifting the apron loop over her head. 'Jenny included. I'm not sure it will be helpful. Not for Jenny. I don't want anything kicking off. Not tonight.'

'It seems to be what Jenny wants.' Henry is still staring at his wife.

'I'm not sure she *knows* what she wants, any more than we do.' She sighs. 'Oh, stuff it. Say yes.' Barbara suddenly throws the apron onto the kitchen work surface. 'It's going to be horrible, whoever is in the house.'

Their conversation is interrupted by a thud upstairs. Jenny's footsteps stamping around her bedroom above the kitchen – all the time shouting into her mobile. Most of it incoherent until they hear, 'God, no. Please . . . no.'

Then a terrible noise of crashing and glass smashing as objects are apparently hurled around the room.

CHAPTER 6

THE WITNESS

'You need to take this straight to the police.'

'That's out of the question.'

'I'm sorry?'

I'm thrown.

I take the latest postcard back, all the while examining Matthew Hill very closely. I had not expected this reaction. I have wrapped this new card in a plastic wallet taken from Luke's school folder. One of those very slippery plastic wallets with holes pre-punched. Dangerous things. I slipped on one left on the floor once and bashed my shoulder really badly.

The latest message arrived like the others, in a plain dark envelope with a printed address label. But this one is even odder and just a little more threatening. Black background again, with the lettering stuck on. KARMA. YOU WILL PAY. To start with I thought it very strange – the link with Buddhism or yoga or whatever. Weren't they about gentleness and kindness and forgiveness? But then I looked it up online and read about karma being interpreted by some people as a kind of natural justice or comeuppance – bad consequence for bad action – and I started to go a bit cold . . .

I have to make this stop.

'I thought you investigated this kind of thing? That's what private investigators do?' I regret the mild sarcasm but I am tense, still staring Matthew Hill right in the eyes, just a little disorientated, too. His advert made it sound straightforward. *Exeter-based PI. Ex-police.* Neat. Simple. I had imagined I would say what I wanted. And he would do it. That this is how he earns his living. Like someone coming into my shop. *Birthday bouquet, please. Certainly.*

'Look. I've been following the coverage. This is new evidence. The girl's still missing, and when there is a live inquiry I have this rule that I don't—'

'Trust me, Mr Hill, this is *not* evidence.'

'And you know this because . . . ?'

I pause for a moment, not at all sure how much I should share.

'Look. I know who this is from. It's from the girl's mother, Barbara Ballard. She's very upset with me. No. That's an understatement. She is beyond upset, and who can blame her. I certainly don't. I brought this entirely on myself. When the first postcard arrived I admit I considered telling the police. For a moment it really shook me, frightened me. We had quite a lot of hassle after my name was leaked and I thought it was more of the same. But I realise now what this is really about. There have been three, and so I just need you to gently warn her off, please. To stop this. Otherwise my husband will find out and then he will insist we go to the police, which I don't want for her. She's got enough to deal with.'

'Well, I'm afraid I'm with your husband on this. You could well be wrong.'

'Look – she comes to my shop. Twice so far. Just watches me through the window. She doesn't know that I know. Obviously . . .'

'Right. So when did this start?' His expression has changed.

'We're talking in confidence? Yes?'

'Of course.'

'Good – because I am not reporting this, either. It really is my own fault. And I don't just mean about the train. I went down there, you see. To Cornwall, last summer. To see the mother. My husband warned me not to and it turns out he was right. It was completely stupid of me. I see that now. Just one in a long line of mistakes I've made over this whole terrible business. The worst, as you will be well aware, was not phoning . . . not warning that poor family in the first place.'

'You didn't hurt the girl, Mrs Longfield. Weren't there a couple of guys in the picture. Key suspects. Just out of Exeter?'

'Yes. But that makes me feel worse rather than better, Mr Hill.'

'Matthew. Please call me Matthew.'

'*Matthew*. My husband says the same thing over and over. That this is not my fault. But I'm afraid it doesn't make me feel any better. And I can't bear that they haven't found her.'

There is a hissing noise suddenly from an adjoining room. I glance to the door across the office, which is ajar, and Matthew Hill stands suddenly, his expression softening.

'I tell you what. Would you like a coffee, Mrs Longfield? I make a pretty good cappuccino.'

'Ella. And yes, please. It smells as if you know what you're doing.' I feel a smile, relaxing a little, my shoulders changing shape. 'I am rather fond of good coffee.'

'Espresso machine. Imported beans – my own mix. It's a weakness.'

'Mine too.' I take a deep breath. 'Sorry to be so spiky before. I was quite nervous, coming here.'

'Most people are.' His voice trails off as he disappears into what I presume is a flat alongside the office. He is gone for quite some time, eventually reappearing with a tray bearing two coffees plus a jug of foaming milk. I nod to the offer of milk.

'So, tell me some more about this mother. About your visit to Cornwall. All of it. No holding back on me.'

'All right. I don't know how closely you've followed the case but there was an awful kerfuffle with the press when they found out that I was the witness on the train. The nationals got terribly excited. Sent all their feature writers down. Big-moral-dilemma headlines. "What would you have done?" and all that.'

'Yes. I saw the stories.' He leans forward in his chair, sipping at the drink.

'All very unpleasant. I have a flower shop. It was so awful we had to shut it for a month and close our social media accounts, too. I found I couldn't face people. Friends were very understanding but some people were a bit odd. Even regular customers. You could tell from the way they looked at me.'

'I'm sorry. The fallout from cases is underestimated. People can be very unkind.'

'Yes, well. Tony, my husband, was completely furious. Like I say, he is very protective. A sweet man – and he was furious that my name got out.'

'And how exactly did that happen?'

'We were never entirely sure. I was at a floristry conference in South London. Training and business-modelling. Officially the police insist that the press just got lucky and put the jigsaw together by tracing me as one of only two people on the course from Devon. But Tony suspects a deliberate leak to boost press interest in the case.'

Matthew pulls a face.

'So you do think that's possible?' I ask.

'Wouldn't like to say. It seems highly unlikely. They wouldn't want to put you in danger.'

'Danger? So you really think I might be in danger now?'

'Sorry. I didn't mean to alarm you. It's not as if you're the only one who could identify these men. No. I really think it's unlikely there would be a deliberate leak. An accidental one . . . that's a different matter.'

'Well – either way. Everyone knows now. I'm the woman on the train who did nothing.'

'Tough for you, then?'

'Yes. But nothing compared to what that family has been through.'

'So why on earth did you go down there? To Cornwall?'

I can feel the sigh leaving my body and put the coffee down for a moment, cradling my head in my palms. 'Completely stupid of me, I know. But the thing is, when I saw her, Mrs Ballard, outside my shop, just watching me, I recognised her from the press coverage – it was in the local paper such a lot. Anyway. It gave me the creeps, and when I thought it over, I felt it would be better to try to talk to her. I got it into my head that if I told her in person how very, very sorry I was and that I accepted she had the right to be angry – that if she could see that I was a mother, too, and how terrible I felt about her pain . . .'

Matthew's face gives him away.

'Yes. I know. Stupid of me.'

'And she reacted badly?'

'Understatement. She went completely berserk. Of course, I can see it now. I was being selfish. I had this fantasy in my head that if she could just see that I was a decent person and that I so badly regretted—'

'Was anyone else there?'

'No. Just the two of us. I took some flowers. A big posy of primroses, which I read were Anna's favourites – which I can see now was probably the trigger. Made it so much worse. She became quite hysterical. Said she was sick of flowers and I had no place. No right. Floral tributes as if her daughter were dead. Which she doesn't believe she is, incidentally.'

Matthew pours some more frothy milk into his coffee and offers me the same, but I put my hand over the cup.

'Do you think it's possible? That the girl is still alive?'

Matthew tightens his lips. 'Possible, but statistically unlikely.'

'That's what we think. Me and Tony.' For a moment my voice falters. I wish that I could feel more hopeful. I think of a recent television drama in which missing girls were found years later. I try to picture Anna emerging from a basement or a hiding place with a police blanket around her shoulders, but I cannot shape the scene in my mind. I cough, looking away to the wall of filing cabinets and then back, picking up my coffee cup once more. 'So anyway. It was pretty terrible in Cornwall. I tried to leave. Apologising for disturbing her. She rather lost it.'

'Physically?'

'She wasn't herself.'

'Did she hurt you, Ella? I mean, if she hurt you, if she's volatile, then you really ought to go to the police with this. They should know this.'

'She didn't mean to. A tussle on the steps outside – an accident more than anything. Just a bit of bruising. On my arm.'

Matthew is now shaking his head.

'Oh, for goodness sake; it was my own fault. She's not a violent woman. It wasn't deliberate and I should never have gone there. Provoked her. But the point is, it shook me up a bit. I mean – I knew that she blamed me and I wanted to try to redress that. But the extent of her hatred. Her eyes.'

'Which is why you think the postcards are from her.'

'Don't you?'

He shrugs, tilting his head from side to side.

'I wish you had kept them all.'

'Sorry. I didn't want my husband to worry. He's going for a promotion at work and has enough on his plate. Look, Mr Hill. Sorry – Matthew. If you won't take this on for me, I will burn them. I'm not handing them in to the police, I can tell you that.'

Matthew examines my face very closely and shifts position.

CHAPTER 15

THE WITNESS

Sometimes people ask me, *Why flowers, Ella?*

The truth is I cannot remember when life, for me, wasn't about flowers. Right from when I was tiny and I used to collect wild flowers on walks with my gran, mesmerised by the colours and the scents and the way you could make the whole impact and mood change by combining them in different ways. The simple, joyful sunburst of a huge fistful of primroses, then the softening and mellowing effect if you added in just a few bluebells for the surprise, the contrast. The hint of the Mediterranean, with the blue and the yellow together.

I would so love it when my mother let me pick flowers from the supermarket to put in vases at home, experimenting with the way they fell. Learning how tulips only look right if you put them in precisely the right height of vase so they weep over the rim. Not too much. Not too little.

I have never forgotten the joy of learning to revive roses with fresh water and cutting the stems super sharp at an angle. The miracle of them lifting up their heads again as if saying *thank you*.

It was no surprise that when I was old enough for a Saturday job, I knew precisely where I would try first. There was a small florist in the town I grew up in. I passed it every day on my walk to school, always stopping to examine the buckets of daffodils outside in the spring, glancing at the window displays. It wasn't especially inspirational, to be honest: standard bouquets, standard displays and too many carnations.

But I have never been more proud than when I was offered my regular six-hour Saturday shift. Up early to help sort the new stock, breathing in the heavenly scent of it all. The shiny ribbon. The rustle of tissue and cellophane. I learned very quickly to respect the popular tastes – the horror of those carnations and the ugly ferns. I was careful not to offend, biting my tongue at first. But as my confidence and my knowledge grew, I started to make little suggestions to our regulars. *How about sunflowers? Or lilies? Something a bit different for a change?*

And it wasn't long before the manager, Sue, allowed me to order in new things, and to make up my own little set-price bouquets.

You have a really good eye, Ella. You're a natural . . . You should do a course.

So I did. A basic course for starters, then a second, more advanced course for wedding flowers, and a third for contemporary design. After that I entered a competition and made the local paper by winning a regional award.

The prize was a week working with a top florist in London, visiting the flower markets at the crack of dawn. Scary. Exhausting. Exhilarating. Heaven . . .

And then the unimaginable. After I had finished A levels, I did a year at college: floristry and business studies. During that year, my grandmother died, leaving an unexpected legacy to be shared between her five grandchildren. *Go travelling*, said my friends. *Blow it on a car. Or a world trip.*

No. Lying in bed at night, beaming, I knew exactly what I wanted to do.

I managed to negotiate the lease on this place. A shop of my own. Complete madness, my parents said. *Do you have any idea how many small businesses fail in their first year?*

And yes – they were right, in a way. It took much longer to come good than I expected. In truth, it provided little more than the minimum wage after costs, in that first year, and let's not talk about the hours I put in. But it *didn't* fail – quite the opposite by the time I got into my stride, in the second and third years.

I learned how to make the bread-and-butter earnings from weddings and seasonal holidays. Mother's Day. Valentine's Day. But the devil was definitely in the detail, I was sure of that.

To compete with the supermarkets, I knew I had to offer something distinctive. My floral USP was an informal, shabby-chic style, with homemade touches that set us apart. My bouquets were hand-tied before this was common practice. I used unusual twine, and handmade labels decorated with pressed flowers from blooms that had gone over.

I learned to waste nothing. Discounted posies when I'd over-ordered. Spent extra hours with the flower presses to ensure no waste.

Soon I was selling little cards and labels, as well as using them on my bouquets. A very useful extra-income stream.

And so this is where I am happiest. My shop. My creation.

Here in the shop I do not worry so much what people think of me or what I say – whether I am old-fashioned or an old head on young shoulders, which is what everyone used to say when I set this place up.

Here – where it is just 6 a.m. and the rest of the world is barely stirring – I am in my own little world, with orders to make up before we meet with the police back at the house. Back in the real world, where Anna is still missing and the postcards have started to frighten Tony as well as me.

I work carefully. A birthday bouquet to be collected at noon. Six table decorations for a dinner at one of the local hotels. Two cups of coffee. Three.

I work carefully, using my favourite secateurs. Bright red handles with the sharpest blade on the market. Superb.

And then the strangest thing. At around six thirty, maybe six forty-five, I leave the last of the table decorations on the counter, nearly finished, to use the loo, which is a tiny extension at the back of the unit. When I return to the bench, the secateurs are gone.

There is the noise of a car right outside and, I admit it, I am spooked. Thrown by this. I am normally so very careful with the secateurs, you see, not just because they are dangerous but because they are extremely expensive. I don't want them to drop on the floor. For the handles to crack. They are a bit like a chef's favourite knife. A lucky charm. I have two spare sets in the drawers but I don't feel comfortable using any others. They just don't feel the same in my hand.

I walk to the front door and stare out to the parking area outside. A single car has its headlights on full beam so I can't see who is inside. I check the shop door. Unlocked. But then I don't normally worry about this. Whenever I am here, I consider myself open for business. If anyone spots the lights on and calls in early, I want to *sell*. Will always take an order. But today, just this once, I put the latch across the top. I stand very still and find that my heart is pumping. I wait a while. Two minutes. Maybe more.

Don't be so silly, Ella. Don't overthink this.

And then the car finally pulls away and I feel my shoulders move, reminding myself that the neighbouring shops have flats above them and this is not so surprising. This early movement. Probably just someone off to work?

So I return to the workbench area at the back of the shop and am totally confused. From this new angle through the archway to the serving area at the front, I can see the secateurs resting on the top of the till. I honestly don't remember putting them there. Can't ever remember putting them there before. There is a slight slope to the top of the till, and this doesn't seem the kind of thing I would do at all. What if they were to slide off?

I look around me in the way you look around the kitchen when you can't find the ingredient you thought you had removed already from the fridge.

I am tired. That's it. *You are tired and you are on edge. Overthinking and messing up, Ella. Tony was right . . . you should have stayed home and done this later.*

Way too many thoughts pumping around my brain. I finish up the final decoration quickly and store everything in the cooler near the workbench – a sort of flower-fridge that keeps everything at the perfect temperature, all ready for my return.

Back at the house, Tony is in the kitchen in his dressing gown.

'You OK? I've been worried. You should have let me come with you.'

'It was fine. I wanted you here to speak to Luke. All done.'

His tone is just a little calmer now, but I can tell from the way he is standing, and also the dark shadows under his eyes, that he has not slept much either. He reacted just as I expected, more worried than cross. *You should have told me, Ella. No more secrets . . .*

Which makes me feel terrible. I showed him the most recent postcard. But I haven't mentioned Matthew yet . . .

'I don't know how I feel about you working at the shop on your own now. Early like this, I mean. Until we know precisely what is going on. What the police say. I wish you had listened to me. Stayed home. Or let me come with you.'

'I had to get the orders done, Tony. And anyway, it will just turn out to be some saddo. A spotty teenager with nothing better to do.' I cannot make this sound entirely convincing, because I no longer know what I think. What I believe. How scared I really ought to be.

'They called at the house, Ella. Whoever wrote that card called here. At the house.'

'Yes. And you're right – it changes things, and I realise now that I should have told you right at the beginning and I'm very sorry about that. But I am happy to take advice now. The police are going to be here in half an hour. I'll listen to whatever they say, Tony. The only reason I wasn't worried before is I honestly thought it was the mother.'

'But can we rethink you working early on your own?'

'If it will make you happier, I can try to juggle a bit in the future.' I look him in the face. 'So did you speak to Luke?'

Last night in bed, Tony was the one to say it first. *Would you think I was mad if I said we should offer to adopt the baby?* I cried and hugged him tight, so relieved that he was thinking exactly the same thing as me. We agreed we are too old and it is probably completely insane, but there is no way we could let someone else bring up Luke's child if Emily's family can't cope.

'He says he'll mention it to Emily later. She's only ten weeks, so it's a bit early for decisions.' Tony puts his hand up to my cheek. 'I think he was relieved, but it's hard to tell. He's still in shock.'

Tony goes on to say Luke would like to stop working at the shop down the line. He's finding it too much with all the worrying. I completely understand, though I know it won't be easy to find a replacement. The early starts put people off. But Luke must come first, so we will have to work something out.

'OK. So let's see what the police have to say, shall we? Talk again about Luke and the shop after that.' I take his hand, still rested on my cheek, and kiss it.

To be honest, I am surprised that we are to see the London DI. Apparently he is down for an update with the Ballards in Cornwall, so will be calling in here on the way back.

Matthew has updated me. His police-contact friend handed over the earlier postcard. Nothing from forensics. No prints. But they want to see this new one, too. I have put it in a transparent freezer bag. Matthew says they will provide proper evidence bags and special gloves for me to use if any more postcards turn up. Better chance of getting prints, apparently. He has asked me not to mention him by name. To imply that I handed the postcards over to the police myself.

Tony has now stepped away and is looking under the sink, I assume for fly spray; there's a bluebottle buzzing at the kitchen window. Eventually he gives up on the cupboard and instead opens the window to shush the fly out with a piece of kitchen towel, before turning back to me and tilting his head.

'You look really tired, Ella. You doing all right, love?'

'I'm fine. Just relieved you know about the postcards now.'

CHAPTER 16

THE FATHER

Henry is sitting at a favourite spot on the stone wall, which has an overview of the higher, troublesome fields. There is just a little mist still hovering around the river below, but the sheep are safely across the other lane and Sammy is happy. Henry smooths the dog's ears.

It is moments like this, watching the early sun burning off the mist, that he feels the most calm. He is thinking that he would like to put in some more fencing lower down in the largest of these fields, to keep the sheep from the muddy slope down to the river. But fencing is expensive. And Barbara is not up for spending on the farm.

New kitchens and new power showers for the holiday cottages? Bring it on. Paying some web designer to upgrade their search engine optimization, whatever that means? That apparently *makes sense financially*. But fencing? Feed? Tractor repairs?

Henry looks down at the dog, whose tongue is lolling as he pants from the joy of checking the boundaries of this field. And the one next door.

To Henry, this is what makes real sense still. A dog who happily races around the perimeter of every field he visits, returning to his master with a triumphant wag of the tail and meeting of the eyes to confirm that all boundaries have been checked.

Henry glances at his watch. An hour to go. He ought to get back. Have a shower. Have another row with Barbara. Try one final time to calm things down before he faces the music proper.

Come on then, boy.

He deliberately takes the long way round. Cannot face Primrose Lane today. Back at the house he is still in the boot room, hanging up his wax jacket, when Barbara appears.

'Where have you been? We need to talk some more, Henry. Before the police get here. I'm worried how much trouble I'll be in. We need to think of Jenny.'

'I'll come through.'

In the kitchen, she sits at the large scrubbed-pine table, drumming her fingers. He stares at the kettle alongside the Aga, wondering about a cup of tea, but thinks better of it. Looks back at his wife.

'I could be in serious trouble, Henry. I knew I should never have let you persuade me to lie to the police.' She is pulling at the sleeve of her jumper, stretching it and then turning back the cuff.

'It will be all right, Barbara. We're setting it all straight. They will understand.'

'Will they? Will they really?'

Henry closes his eyes. He is sorry that he has upset his wife. He is sorry that she is going through this on top of everything else. That he is a bad husband. But he is also very tired of having to say sorry a million times over, because it doesn't help or change anything.

'I'm sorry, Barbara.'

'Well, with respect, it's a bit late for that now. It's perjury, isn't it, to lie to the police?'

'I think that's just in court, love.'

Henry looks down at the floor. At his thick, grey woollen socks.

You disgust me. Anna's voice again. In his head. In his car. In the passenger seat, refusing to look him in the face.

And in this moment he realises that there isn't anything Barbara can say or the police can say to possibly make him feel worse than he already does.

'I still don't understand why we had to lie, anyway. I mean – do you have any idea, Henry, how it was for me that night, eh? Here on my own. Our daughter missing. Me here . . . all on my own.'

Henry closes his eyes and says nothing.

'And by the way, I want you to move out.'

'Oh, come on, Barbara. How is that going to help? Think of Jenny. And how am I going to keep the farm going if I move out?'

'There is no farm, Henry. There hasn't been a farm for years.'

He opens his eyes and meets hers.

'And you wonder why this isn't working out, Barbara? You marry a farmer and then you decide that you don't want to be married to a farmer.'

'That isn't fair.'

'Isn't it?'

They sit for several minutes, saying nothing at all.

'Right. So we see them together – the police, Barbara. And I explain why I asked you to lie the night Anna went missing. It will be fine. We'll iron it out. I'm sorry I have upset you, but if you really want me to move out, then with respect I think what I do after today stops being any of your business. For now, I am going to have a shower before they arrive.'

Upstairs, under the stream of water which he turns up too hot deliberately, Henry feels the relief of it for the first time. The letting go, finally. For years he has allowed himself the delusion that he can keep going like this.

But now?

Henry turns his face up into the stream of water and has to adjust the temperature as the jet burns the tender skin. And for a short time he does what he hasn't done since his mother died. In the stream of the hot water that turns his flesh just a little bit too red, Henry Ballard cries.

He cries for Anna, who will never be found. And who knows the worst of him.

You disgust me, Dad . . .

Afterwards, Henry shaves for the second time that day, selects a blue checked shirt, a clean pair of jeans and a navy sweatshirt. He does all of this on automatic pilot. He is long past the stage of trying to work out some script in his head. It will be what it will be.

When they arrive, there are three of them. A local DS called Melanie Sanders they have met a few times before and who seems quite nice; Cathy, their family liaison officer; and the tall, slim DI from London whom Henry has never liked.

From the off, the mood is markedly different from previous encounters. Cathy accepts the offer of coffee, which Barbara brings to the table on a tray, but the DI declines.

'I understand you want to speak to us, Mr Ballard?'

'Yes. I'm sorry. I feel very bad about this but I need to explain something about the night Anna went missing. I have something I want to clear up.'

The DI glances at the two women police officers and back at the Ballards.

'Interesting – we must be telepathic, you and me, Mr Ballard. Because I came all the way down here to talk to you about *precisely* the same thing.' He does not even try to disguise the sarcasm in his tone or the little twist of the knife.

'You see, we had some very interesting calls after the anniversary appeal on television. Calls which we have found a little bit confusing.'

Henry looks at Barbara, whose expression is frozen.

'So why don't you go first, Mr Ballard.'

'OK. So this is embarrassing. But I lied about the night Anna went missing, and I asked Barbara to back me up because I was so embarrassed. And I didn't want it to distract from your investigation.'

Henry can feel his wife's stare burning into him.

'This is completely my fault. Not my wife's. I had a few too many to drink. I wasn't at home.'

'Not at home?'

'No.'

'And you telling us this now, changing your story, wouldn't have anything to do with the fact that you realise that we have new information?'

'No. Of course not. How would I even know that?'

'OK, Mr Ballard. So this new version of where you were the night your daughter went missing. Will it go any way to explaining how your car was seen near the railway station that evening?'

'Excuse me?'

'Because, Mr Ballard, I am here today to ask you how it is that your car was seen on the evening of Anna's disappearance near Hexton railway station. Not here at the farm, as you and your wife both told us previously. But near a railway station with a fast train to London. So my question is this. Did you go to London the night your daughter disappeared, Mr Ballard? Is that what you really want to tell us?'

'Don't be ridiculous. Of course I didn't. I was here the following morning. When we were liaising with the police. You know I was. That wouldn't be possible. It's too far. How could I possibly—'

'Do you know what, Mr Ballard? On reflection, I think it might be better if we continue this a little more formally. At the local police station. DS Melanie Sanders will give us access to one of her nice interview suites, I'm sure.'

Henry can feel a terrible panic rising within him. A sort of change of temperature which sweeps right through his body. His mind is in such turmoil that for a moment he cannot tell whether he feels too hot or too cold. Just somehow all wrong in the clothes he is wearing. The fabric too close to his skin. Clinging, as if he is still wet from the shower.

In the midst of this panic he looks at his wife, but there is no support or comfort there. Only terrible and wild confusion in her eyes.

'Shall we go then, Mr Ballard?'

Henry thinks that perhaps he should ask whether he has a choice. Whether this is an arrest—or a request. Whether he should get Barbara to phone their lawyer? Dig his heels in and actually refuse to go? But then he quickly regroups, thinking that he needs to be very, very careful. Saying the wrong thing or being uncooperative now could go very badly for him. Could be entirely misunderstood.

And so Henry Ballard stands, and as they walk outside he tries to calm himself, and decides, for now at least, to say nothing more at all.

CHAPTER 17

THE WITNESS

I have been lying in bed thinking about karma. Silly, I know, but that postcard has really gotten under my skin.

I keep having these mixed-up dreams. Anna on the train. The noise of Sarah and her bloke in that wretched toilet cubicle. And then the shock over Luke and his girlfriend.

I'm not one for popcorn psychiatry normally, but you can't miss the irony, can you. And it just feels – I don't know – as if everything in my life is trying to teach me some terrible lesson and my brain just can't cope.

Some nights it gets so bad I get this tight feeling in my chest. Then I have to get up and make a cup of tea and then, of course, Tony gets up too – worried sick – which is the last thing I want. Spreading the guilt. What I try to do is go over it in my mind when I am on my own, playing rewind to think over and over and over about exactly how responsible I am for whatever happened to that poor girl. Wishing so much that I could go back and play it differently.

And then? The problem is, hand on heart, I still cannot go back there in my mind's eye and be anything other than appalled at the thought of that girl and that man having sex in that toilet so soon after they met.

I wish that I could bounce this off people properly. Ask them openly what they would have done. Whether they would be shocked or upset to be confronted by what I heard. The problem is that the police have only ever released information that the 'witness' overheard the girls being chatted up by the guys just out of prison, and that the 'witness' was shocked at how quickly they became close. How quickly they made unwise plans together. Dangerous plans.

I've been judged for that and that alone. For not stepping in because two country girls were being so clearly targeted by two guys with records. That's what all the social media and tabloid press has been about. *What would you have done? Would you have minded your own?* Two sixteen-year-old girls. Two guys just out of prison.

The police have never released the detail of the sex in the toilet, and asked me to keep it quiet for reasons of evidence, so I have only ever been able to tell Tony. He says I was right to be shocked – and that people would keep their noses out of it if they knew all the facts.

We've talked it over again since this business with Luke and his girlfriend, and Tony says it's very different – a young girl having sex with a virtual stranger in a public toilet, and Luke and Emily making a mistake in a caring relationship. I know he's right, but I still feel a bit hypocritical now for judging Sarah so very harshly.

He's gone into work early today, my Tony. He's in retail himself, but a very different sector – selling cereals to supermarkets. He's acting regional manager and is up for the job permanently if his sales figures hit their target. I'm terribly proud of him, though it's a lot of pressure and I wish he didn't have to do so much travelling.

For now, with him away so much, I have promised to juggle my working hours so that I am not alone at the shop out of hours too much. At least not until we hear from the police and feel a bit steadier.

So this feels odd for me. A second cup of coffee in bed. It's 8 a.m., which for a florist amounts to a lie-in. I am having a really good think.

About karma.

Also, whether I am a prude. I mean, I certainly hold my hands up to being a bit out of touch. Naive to imagine that my seventeen-year-old son wouldn't be having sex yet. More and more I keep testing myself, worrying that I am a hypocrite over what happened on the train. Was my judgement about gender? Because my first thought was that Sarah clearly wasn't as 'nice' a girl as I had imagined, which is why I stepped away from the whole situation. Yet if it had been Luke? No. On reflection, maybe not so hypocritical, because I would still be totally appalled and shocked if a son of mine, or any young man, had done that with someone they had just met.

Maybe the truth is that I just like some boundaries. Because don't get me wrong, this is not about sex, per se; Tony and I get along very well in that department ourselves, thank you very much. I just think it's *private*. Sex. Not something casual; something to be talked about with strangers at dinner parties. And certainly not something to share with a complete stranger in a train toilet.

As for karma . . .

But now my mobile is ringing – the display confirms it's Matthew Hill. I check my watch. Ten past eight.

'Hello, Matthew. I was going to ring you, actually. To let you know that the London DI has postponed; he's coming round later now. Has had to stay on in Cornwall for a bit. Some development with the inquiry, he said, which I am hoping means progress.'

'Well, I hate to disillusion you, but I'm afraid you can hold that thought. I've just spoken to my contact down in Cornwall and apparently the investigation is suddenly all over the place. Going right up a blind alley, from what I hear. But never mind that. Big news. I just got *the call*. My wife's gone into labour. I'm on my way to collect her right now. Feels a bit surreal, actually, but I just wanted to check in to let you know I may be out of the loop for a few days.'

'A few days?' I laugh. 'You may just have underestimated this, Matthew. But what lovely news. Please do let me know how it goes. Do you know if it's a boy or a girl yet?'

'No. Goodness. We don't mind . . .'

'OK. Good luck. Drive carefully and try to calm down.'

'I'll be in touch.'

And then I put the phone down and find that I am stilled. Matthew Hill clearly does not have a clue what is coming, and maybe that's not such a bad thing.

Because once you become a parent, you learn that love can involve more fear than you had ever imagined, and you never quite look on the world in the same way again. Which is precisely why I cannot cope with my part in Anna's disappearance.

CHAPTER 18

THE FRIEND

'So is it OK if I bring them through, love? Just for five or ten minutes? Might cheer you up. Nurse says she can make an exception so long as we keep it short.'

Sarah looks at her mother and knows that this is not really a question. Her mother has a very specific expression when she is shaping a recommendation as a question. She leans forward slightly, doesn't blink and then raises her eyebrows, signalling that only the correct answer will actually be heard. Namely – *yes*. As a young child, Sarah would rail against this tactic, but she learned long ago that resistance is futile. And she has no energy for more lectures.

'OK. But I'm feeling tired, so not for long.'

It's day six, and Sarah has been reassured that her liver function is improving. The consultant is looking a good deal less concerned when he pops by the bed, and nurses now say that *everything is going in the right direction*. The psych team are finally off her back and there is even talk of her going home soon.

Sarah is not sure how she feels about going home. She is still reeling from how quickly her emotions shift from hour to hour. How she has so swiftly moved on from fear of death to impatience with the hospital and her mother.

And the other big bogey is back – worrying what will have come out of the television appeal.

The friends troop into the room looking cowed. Sarah is now in a side room just off the general children's ward. At seventeen, she does not qualify for an adult ward, so this provision is to make her feel less awkward. Away from the babies. The nurses have told her she is 'lucky' that this side room was free.

Lucky?

'We didn't know what to bring so we decided on sugar. Your mum won't approve, but hey.' Tim is holding a little carton of biscuits and a box of fudge.

Sarah decides she will punish them all for as long as possible, and refuses to look anyone in the eye.

Just last night she dreamed about them all at the farm, a birthday party Mrs Ballard threw for Tim. He must have been ten, maybe eleven. Anna's mum had been horrified when she discovered Tim's mother didn't bother with parties, and made this huge fuss – a big tea and a star-shaped chocolate cake with fresh cream. Tim and Paul brought a balloon-modelling kit and learned how to make sausage dogs, swords and hats. Walking along the narrow road from the farm to get her lift home after the party, she'd had a bright yellow sausage dog tucked under her arm. She had been so happy that day and so sad it was over. She had felt her expression changing; the two boys looking at her sideways. *Always hard to go home, isn't it?* She can't remember who said it, Tim or Paul, but she remembers exactly how she felt as she nodded – sad, but sort of guilty, too. She knew it was wrong to prefer Anna's family to her own, but she just couldn't help it.

And now? Sarah finally looks up and glances from face to face. She wonders what on earth happened to them all. When exactly did they stop being who they were to each other back then?

Jenny looks pale, and Sarah finds herself hoping she is remembering the horrible things she said during their row. It wasn't just the two boys who were cruel. But then a picture of Anna in the club flashes into Sarah's mind, and she closes her eyes and leans back on her many pillows.

'Sorry. Are you feeling all right? Do we need to get a nurse?' Jenny's voice.

'I'm fine. Just tired.'

'Right, yes. Of course. Look, we promised your mum we wouldn't stay long but we just wanted . . .' Jenny's voice trails off and she suddenly sucks in air.

'Look, we came because we wanted to say sorry. For what we said.' It is Tim who has stepped forward.

Sarah opens her eyes and looks again from one to the other. Tim. Paul. Jenny.

'We just felt so guilty. For swanning off to do other stuff. That's the truth.' Paul is fidgeting with his belt buckle. 'We shouldn't have taken it out on you.'

'You're sorry you said it . . . but you still think it's my fault?'

Sarah keeps her gaze on the boys. They had been the most outspoken when they had the row.

'It's those men. If they could just find those men.' Jenny again.

Finally, Sarah takes a deep breath. 'So – how did the TV appeal go? Many calls? I've got my phone back but not enough data to see it.'

The ice broken, they babble about how much the appeal helped. Loads of calls, apparently. Sarah lies again and says the pills really were an accident and they're not to worry.

'So you won't do it again?' Jenny's tone is urgent.

'No. I won't. I promised my mum I would be more careful, and I couldn't put her through that again. It was completely stupid. So tell me then. This TV appeal. What exactly did they show?'

Jenny says that she's really pleased they used the lovely video of Anna, and also one of the photographs that she emailed the producer of the programme, but her mother was upset that her interview had been cut back so dramatically.

'They edited out all the bits of her talking about other missing girls who have turned up and her saying that no one should give up hope – that any piece of information might be key to finding Anna alive.'

Everyone is silent for a moment.

Sarah closes her eyes again.

And then her mother is suddenly back in the room, ushering everyone out and saying that the staff have bent the rules and they don't want to push their luck.

They each say goodbye and sorry, yet again.

After they have gone, Sarah's mother sits on the chair next to the bed and fidgets. She smooths her skirt over and over.

'What's the matter, Mum?'

'Nothing.'

'Yes, there is.'

Her mother pours some cordial into Sarah's empty glass and tops it up with water from the plastic jug. She examines the box of fudge as if reading the description on the back.

'OK. So the police have been in touch again, Sarah. And of course the doctors say you are too poorly to see them. I wanted to keep this from you. You've been through quite enough but apparently they do want another little chat with you once you're home, so I thought you should know. Prepare yourself. So it doesn't set you back.'

'What about? What do they want to talk to me about?'

'Apparently there have been some more witnesses from the club. After the TV appeal. That's all I know.'

'But I've told them everything. Everything I know.'

'I know, love.'

'No. I don't want to talk to them again.'

'OK, love. I understand. No need to upset yourself. I'll try to explain to them that you need to rest.'

And now Sarah is leaning back on her pillows, closing her eyes and trying once again to block out the echo of Anna's voice. The desperation on her face that night in the club.

Please, Sarah. I don't feel safe. I'm begging you. Please . . .

CHAPTER 19

THE WITNESS

About that promise I made to Tony not to do any more early stints at the shop on my own until the new alarms are installed . . . Well. You try getting a depressed teenage boy out of bed at the crack of dawn.

It's hard to be too cross. Luke promised he'd keep up the job until we find a replacement, but he wanders round like a zombie now. Always looks so tired. We're letting him stay off school for a few more days while everyone adjusts to what's going on with Emily. But it's hard to know how to play it.

This morning I banged on his door early, but no answer. I checked later and he just looked terrible. Bad headache, too – so I gave him some tablets and asked him to join me when he can. Tony is in Bristol so I have a dilemma. Duty to my customers versus safety and my promise to Tony. The only upside is the police have been pretty good. It's probably guilt for letting my name get out. They've been sending a patrol car past the house and shop every so often just to bump up 'presence'. They seem pretty sure it's just a saddo, but we're getting new alarms for the shop anyway, and I'm trying to tell myself it is all covered now.

The bottom line is that I decide to pop in early on my own – just this once – and will keep pestering Luke. He passed his test recently and Tony got him a Mini, so he can zip down in that once he's up to it.

By the time I arrive at the shop, I've messaged Luke twice more but had no reply yet. To be honest, I'm sad he wants to give up the job. Luke has been helping out at weekends since he was about fourteen; he used to be so keen and he's good with the customers. It made sense all round – it's extra money for him and I feel it instils a bit of discipline. Plus understanding what it actually feels like to be paid by the hour – both the slog of it and also the satisfaction when the day is done.

Tony's trip to Bristol is important vis-à-vis this promotion – they're deciding if they should rebrand their cereals – and I've decided I won't let him know about this. He'll get upset and worry about me being on my tod here in the dark.

So. *Concentrate, Ella.* I'm up against it. Six table decorations for a lunch at the town hall. It's a good gig and quite a regular booking through a catering contact, so I don't like to let them down. That's the problem with repeat business: on the one hand, you're grateful for it and flattered, but on the other, you're always dreading that you might become dependent on it. Terrified to put a foot wrong in case the client goes somewhere else.

I normally draw up sketches and a mood board and agree those via email with the catering manager Kate. She's got a good eye herself and often posts pictures of my stuff on social media, which all helps these days. I've earned quite a reasonable reputation with her for doing something a bit different. So I don't like to slip up or get complacent.

Part of the whole drive to keep what I do looking fresh has been building up a good range of vases and props, so that I can really ring the changes. I just wish I had more storage space, though if I'm brutally honest, I probably spend too much on presentation. It's a fine line with a business as small as mine, but I think investing in kit helps win repeat business, and it's important to constantly surprise clients. It certainly leads to more photo shares on social media.

For this job, I'm using small galvanised-steel buckets; we've agreed an ultra-modern but vibrant look. I'm going with red anthuriums, white roses and Eustoma, against really glossy green foliage. It will look very striking with the white tablecloths and neutral room.

I'm always telling Tony that what you hope for with every order is that guests will ask, *Who did the flowers?* Kate is very loyal and always keeps my cards available. The only frustration for me is when conference delegates get in touch from far afield offering new work, as I can only cater within a certain radius.

Goodness. Time's going on and no word from Luke.

It's still quite dark and I'm thinking about another cup of coffee when I hear a car engine. I wonder if it's Luke, but I'm not sure it sounds like his Mini. The car pulls up outside. It stops. I stop.

Ridiculous. *It's just a car, Ella. Calm yourself.*

I stand very still, waiting for the car to move off, but it doesn't. The headlights go out. I tell myself it is probably someone for one of the flats.

I wait a minute or two and text Luke again. No answer. All is quiet now and so I turn back to the anthuriums. I tell myself to concentrate on the flowers. And then . . . Oh my goodness.

Someone is trying the door handle of the shop. It's locked, of course. *Christ.*

Luke has a key. It can't be Luke.

I pick up my mobile, ready to dial for help. I am thinking that if whoever's there forces their way in, I will run through the back and dial the police as I do so. Even as this plan takes shape in my head, I feel both ridiculous and simultaneously afraid.

There is more rattling of the door handle. I can't see who's there because of the blind drawn down over the glass section.

I keep very still. The only lights on in the shop are in the rear workbench area. I'm not going to the door. No way. There is a part of me that wants to believe it is Luke – that he has forgotten his key. But he would call out to me, surely?

Footsteps. Yes. Finally, I can hear someone walking away outside. Good. Good. Thank God. The car lights back on now. Driving off.

I wonder if I should phone Tony but then remember I'm not meant to be here on my own.

It is so odd that you can stand in a space – a place in which you normally feel so happy and safe – and then suddenly you can stand in precisely the same spot and feel like this completely different person.

I don't want to be this person.

I hate this new person.

I can actually feel tears coming now. And what I am thinking is, *You stupid, stupid woman. Why didn't you just do the right thing a year back? Give the parents a call when you were on that train and make this all their responsibility – their call – and not yours?*

Why, why, why? *Why didn't you do that one, simple thing, Ella?*

I don't know how long I have been standing here, but a glance at the big clock on the wall tells me it's too long. I am seriously up against it now.

Then my mobile rings and I jump right out of my skin. Luke's name.

'Were you just at the door?'

'No. What do you mean? I'm ringing to say I'm just setting off. But why so spooked, Mum?'

'Nothing. Nothing. Look, will you just get down here as soon as you can. You promised your dad . . .'

I hang up. And instantly regret my tone. Damn. I send a text to apologise.

Sorry. Just tired. Coffee machine is on.

And then I finally get back to the flowers and try to let myself soak up the brilliant colours and the scent. Concentrate on the work.

For a moment, I wonder if I have made the wrong choice with the buckets. Should I have gone for the mirrored square containers instead? No – it's too late anyway. I don't have time to start again. This will be fine.

It is light outside now, which is a huge relief as I can see the cars passing and parking more clearly without the blinding headlights. I no longer feel that ridiculous sense of being watched, as though I'm in a goldfish bowl.

Nearly 7 a.m. and the door rattles again. This time a text from Luke to confirm it's him. He really has forgotten his keys.

'Why do you lock the door, Mum? I thought you liked it when you got some impromptu trade.'

'Dad said it was a good idea. With these stupid postcards someone's sending.'

'I thought the police said it was probably some random saddo.'

'They did. And it probably is. But we just want to be a bit careful. You know, just to be on the safe side. How's your headache?'

'Gone. So – will you have to see them again? The police?' He looks worried, and I wish I had not said so much.

'Don't know. Probably not. It will all settle down again, I'm sure.'

'Well, if I find out who sent those postcards, I'll sort them out.'

'Don't say that, Luke. That's no help – to say things like that. We need to let the police handle it now. Not us.'

'That's not what Dad said.'

'Pardon?'

'Oh, nothing.' He looks sheepish. 'So you want another coffee, Mum? I'm starving, by the way. Got any food?'

CHAPTER 20

THE FATHER

Henry first held a gun in his hand when he was nine.

His father made him promise not to tell his mother. His uncle George was also there that day. They took him down to one of the lower fields, down by the river, to shoot rabbits.

Vermin, his father explained. Seven rabbits could apparently eat as much as a sheep. Hence they were a nightmare for the crops – also the vegetable garden. And their digging caused terrible problems for the livestock, too. Henry's father said that as a child himself he had once seen a calf with a terrible twisted leg after it lost its footing in a rabbit hole. It had to be shot, of course, but it had suffered horribly, crying out in pain, until the gun could be fetched from the locked cabinet. *Wretched rabbits . . .*

Much was made, that first shooting lesson, about the rules and about safety. The licence and the law. Henry was told that he would be allowed to have a shotgun himself when he was a lot bigger, but only when he had proved that he could take responsibility and follow every single rule to the letter. It was both within the law and essential to keep the rabbits under control, but they were not allowed to shoot badgers so it was terribly important to be careful.

His dad and his uncle explained the safety sequence. No livestock. No public access. Only in daylight. Always check that there are no other shooters ahead of you. Make absolutely sure you know where everyone in the party is before you fire.

Lying in the grass, his father set up the gun for him and taught him how it should be fired. He was warned that it would kick back a bit into his shoulder and he should brace himself for that. But he would soon get used to it. They would take him to a shooting range and to clay pigeon shooting, too, to help improve his aim.

First shot and Henry was absolutely horrified. Complete fluke. Instant hit. The shock of seeing the rabbit sort of leap, then fall. His father's amazement and immediate cock-a-hoop celebration were at complete odds with the feeling in Henry's own stomach. He didn't like to say, but a little bit of sick was suddenly in his mouth and he thought he might have to retch.

Well done, son. Seriously well done. A natural. My God, George. You see that? He has a natural eye.

These days the gun cabinet is in the small office alongside the boot room. It meets all the regulations, though Henry wishes he had opted for the model with a combination lock. His basic steel version has a key that he has to store separately. Technically he is not supposed to tell anyone where this is and he is supposed to change its location regularly. In practice, he has more than once forgotten its 'new' secret location, storming around the house and cursing at Barbara and the girls. So his current routine is to keep it in his sock drawer, inside an old pair of red rugby socks he never wears. Henry finds this easy to remember and tells himself a thief is unlikely to rummage through his socks.

Just occasionally there is some drama on the news about a child getting hold of a gun and Henry gets himself in a panic, checking the red socks.

Today, Henry rises early in the sparse sadness of the spare bedroom. Barbara insisted he move out of their shared room the moment he got

119

back from the police station. There was no formal arrest and the police are still checking out his new story, but with Barbara urging him to move out completely, Henry realises that he has made things worse, not better.

So what did they say, the police? Why was your car near the railway station? I thought you said you were drunk. Slept in the pub car park? Why the hell won't you tell me what's going on, Henry . . .

He looks at his watch. 5.30 a.m. He checks the bedside table drawer for the key, which he took from the socks last night while Barbara was making supper. He throws on the same clothes from yesterday, discarded on a chair, and puts the key in his right pocket. Then he draws the curtains, wincing at a sky much too beautiful for this day. This mood. This plan.

Henry listens to his breathing for a little while, staring out at the patterning of the clouds. Cirrostratus. His father taught him about clouds, too. Essential for a farmer to be able to read the clouds. Cirrostratus clouds are like thin, almost transparent sheets on a washing line. They mean rain is on its way, and he feels the familiar, involuntary pull inside. The need to crack on. Get going.

Henry heads downstairs, being careful to be as quiet as possible, avoiding the third step from the bottom, which creaks the loudest. He walks through the kitchen to the boot room, where Sammy is all bright-eyed enthusiasm, wagging his tail.

Henry feels a lurch in his stomach as he meets the familiar amber stare. He pets the dog's head – *stay* – then heads through to the office, taking the key from his pocket. Henry chooses his oldest shotgun, takes ammunition from the back of the wooden filing cabinet in the corner (not strictly very safe but he has let things slip a little), relocks the steel cabinet and walks back through to the boot room, where Sammy still stands, head tilted, waiting for permission.

'No. Not today, boy. You stay here.'

The dog looks bemused. Ears back. He stands proud and moves slightly.

'I said *stay* – you hear? Back in your bed. Now.'

Their eyes meet again and Sammy slinks back into his bed where he sits all beady-eyed, staring and panting, tongue lolling, as Henry leaves the room.

Outside it is cooler than he expected. Henry looks across to the little lawn opposite the drive, remembering once more the tents and the trampoline. The girls shrieking with laughter from a den in the bushes.

He remembers how Anna loved to be swung around by her legs in the middle of the lawn when she was very small. How sad he felt when she became too tall for it to be safe anymore.

You're too tall.

Oh, please, Daddy.

You'll bang your head. I can't.

He remembers the vigil, which had so surprised him. It was quite touching that so many people came. The candles. The singing. Barbara and Jenny standing with their arms linked together, too upset to join in. Their lips tight, so they would not cry.

He looks back up at the house, the curtains all drawn upstairs still, and moves as quietly as he can on the gravel to the adjacent barn. He uses the small side door, leaving the large double doors for the tractor bolted at both top and bottom. He moves into the far corner to sit in the midst of the spare straw bales from the vigil.

Henry places the gun on the ground and feels his heart rate increase. Is he afraid?

No answer comes back.

Instead, a whole album of images plays out in front of him. A pack of cards shuffled and spread. Barbara and him on their honeymoon. Such different people. The girls when they were tiny babies. Anna with her fair hair; Jenny so dark.

Henry wonders if his subconscious is trawling the sentimental memories so that he can convince himself to bottle out. But – no. Very soon the police will find out he was not sleeping in the car because he was drunk. Very soon they, and Barbara, too, will find out the truth.

And then a new thought.

You idiot, Henry.

They will hear the shot from the house. Damn. They will come and they will find him. And they will see. Maybe Jenny, first. Why on earth did he not think of this before?

Henry takes his phone from his pocket, trying to work out a strategy. He could ring the police. Tell them to come. Yes. He could bolt the doors from the inside also, so the police will deal with it. Will this work? Or should he walk some distance from the house? Maybe up to the ridge?

But then someone else will have to find him. Some other poor innocent.

Only now does Henry truly realise that he has not thought this through at all.

Quickly he feels in his pocket for a scrap of paper. A pen? He finds nothing but some old receipts, a small piece of wire and an empty chewing gum packet.

He closes his eyes and feels the frown as he thinks of Anna's friend Sarah and her pills. Did she think it through? Mean it? Did she write a note? How will he explain himself if he doesn't leave a note?

Henry's heart is now beating so very fast that his chest is actually aching. He sets the gun ready – cocking it first with two hands – and then places it back on the floor, pointing at his neck.

For some reason he is thinking of a television drama in which the make-up artist said they used liver to create the blood and the mess of a brain, to make it look realistic. He imagines that he has already pulled the trigger and wonders what it will be like. Nothingness? Or something else? Henry is not at all religious so he does not know what he expects. But he is surprised to find that he is worried about pain.

Henry moves the shotgun slightly to face the ceiling of the barn, and makes a decision. No paper and no note, so he will have to ring. Yes. He takes the phone in his right hand again to make the call to the police.

He has the number of DS Melanie Sanders programmed into the phone, and decides he will speak to her first. He likes her. She seems straight. Decent. So much nicer than the guy from the Met. He hears it ringing. One ring. Two. Three. He prays she will answer. Five. Six. His heart continues to pound as he closes his eyes tightly, praying it will not be some recorded message.

CHAPTER 21

THE FRIEND

Sarah says nothing in the car on the way home while her mother chatters and chatters. She is to stay off school. Take as long as she needs. Build up her strength.

Her mother says she is glad Sarah has made up with her gang of friends, and that she must look to them for support now. No one is blaming anyone. There is to be no more *nonsense*. Why don't they have a pizza night soon? Watch a film?

Sarah is surprised to feel unsteady on her feet as they walk through the front garden. Probably all that time in bed. She looks at the three rose bushes below the sitting room window and notices the large number of blooms. When she was taken from the house in the ambulance she remembers lying on the stretcher and passing the flower bed by the front door. There were no blooms then. Now there are five. No. Six. It feels odd somehow, for this to have changed so quickly.

'Come on then, love. I'll make us a nice cup of tea.'

She doesn't want tea but says nothing.

Inside, she just stands in the sitting room in a kind of daze as her mother puts her small bag on the settee. Sarah looks at it. The tartan holdall. Inside is her make-up pouch, which she used so carefully in

London. Eyeliner, mascara and her favourite lip gloss. She looks at herself in the mirror over the settee. No make-up today. Her eyes look small. Her lips dry.

In the reflection she can see photos in a variety of frames on the pine shelving on the opposite wall. There is a shot of her sitting in a paddling pool and blowing bubbles. Both of her parents are sitting alongside, smiling.

In another picture she is doing a handstand, her skirt flailing to show her white-and-pink spotted pants. She is frowning now, trying to remember who took the picture.

And then she scans along the shelf to see the picture of her sister Lily sitting on a bench on a holiday in France. She looks sad. No – not sad, that's not the right word. She looks sort of distant and disconnected.

Sarah can hear the noise of the kettle through the archway that leads into the kitchen.

'Why did Lily really leave?'

'Sorry. Can't hear you over the kettle.' Her mother moves back into the sitting room, standing and staring at her.

Sarah keeps her eyes on the photograph of her sister. 'Why did Lily really leave us?'

'I don't think this is the time to be talking about all of that. You need to rest, love.'

Sarah tilts her head to the side and then turns to look her mother in the face. She can feel a prickle of tears coming and her bottom lip trembling. She knows how easy it will be for her mother to put the pin back in the grenade as she always does. As Sarah always lets her.

'It was over Dad, wasn't it? It's why he left.'

The blood leaves her mother's face.

'Why do you say that? You know why your father left. We weren't getting along . . . and when things blew up with Lily, it all got a bit—'

'What things blew up?'

125

Sarah hasn't seen her sister in three years. Sometimes Lily phones to check that Sarah is OK, but she hasn't in a while. They are friends on Facebook, but when Sarah checks Lily's page, she hardly recognises her. She is in some kind of hippy phase. Her hair dyed strange colours. Odd clothes. Living in Devon in some strange group set-up. Always posting stuff about crystals and healing. All yoga and candles. Reiki and spelt flour. Sarah still misses her; she cannot believe Lily has not been in touch lately with all this going on. Everything all over the news again.

'I want to know the truth, Mum.'

'Truth? You're making it all sound a bit melodramatic, love. You've been through a lot. You're upset. Your father and me, we just stopped working. That's all. You know that we both still love you.'

Sarah holds her mother's stare and tries very hard to read it, to burn her own gaze deep into her mother's, to trigger the reaction she needs. But the kettle announces it's boiling and her mother looks away.

'I don't want a drink, thank you. I'm going to lie down.'

'How about a sandwich?'

'I said I'm fine.' Sarah grabs the overnight bag from the sofa and marches upstairs, where she closes the bedroom door, leaning her back against it with her hand still on the cold ceramic doorknob. She remembers that Lily picked them out – new doorknobs for the whole house. *It's amazing how much difference small details can make.* It was in the phase when Lily was still talking about going to art college and was forever fired up about some project or another. Their tiny utility room was turned over to all manner of schemes. Felt-making or silk-printing one week; hand-dying of cotton sheets for rag rugs the next.

And then suddenly it all stopped. It was replaced by rows. Shouting and slamming of doors upstairs. Lily playing truant from school. Staying in bed all day. That sad look on her face from the photograph in France.

Sarah checks her watch and moves over to her desk to switch on the lamp, adjusting its arm so that it lights her work area perfectly. She fires up her laptop, impatient as it takes time to load and settle.

Her Facebook page is busy with new messages of support, wishing her well. Most of her friends seem to know she is home from hospital today. Word travels fast. She had to unfriend a lot of people who made unpleasant remarks when Anna first went missing. For a while she considered taking down her profile completely. She still gets the occasional nasty comment linked to a news report, but Sarah tries very hard to ignore them, banning anyone who oversteps the line. The truth is she can't bear what some people say, but worries even more about what might be said behind her back. So she keeps the profile going.

Sarah clicks through to her sister's page, where there is an updated profile pic – the ends of Lily's hair dip-dyed pink now. There's also a new batch of photos of some place she does not recognise: orchards and fields and soft-focus shots of yoga outside at dawn. A large group of people, arms linked, their faces turned away from the camera.

Sarah opens up a message to her sister and feels a lurch of sadness. The last time they chatted was not long after it all happened. She rereads all their messages. Lily had called a few times but Sarah was still in shock back then and had clammed up.

Now she feels very differently. She twists her mouth to one side and types. **I need to speak to you, Lily . . .** She is about to press send when she scans the message again, frowning and realising it is too vague; it's not enough to provoke a response. She adds her new mobile number and then types some more . . . **It's about Dad. I'm worried he had something to do with Anna . . .**

She leaves her finger poised over the send button, her heart pounding. For a moment she is not sure that she can do it. She doesn't know whether she has the courage to finally pull the pin from the grenade. She puts both hands up to her mouth momentarily.

And then she lets out a huff of breath and presses send.

CHAPTER 22

THE PRIVATE INVESTIGATOR

'You seriously need to stop looking at me like that.' Matthew's wife is grinning at him, their new daughter sucking happily at her left breast. The baby, impossibly tiny but with an impressive mop of dark hair, has been gently laid on a pillow to shield Sally's stomach after the caesarean.

Matthew cannot help it. His mouth is gaping, his eyes wide. It's still all so . . .

'I'm sorry. I just can't take it in.'

'I know. *It's a miracle*, as you keep telling me, Matt. And I love that you're like this, I really do. But you have to stop looking at me with that face.'

'What face?'

'The worship face. As if I'm suddenly some kind of goddess. It's spooking me. Even more than your sex face.'

'There is nothing wrong with my sex face.' He pokes out his tongue.

Matthew is not about to admit that he actually checked out his sex face – in the bathroom mirror – in a fit of pique and paranoia, after his wife mentioned in the early days of their relationship that it was quite *interesting*. No one had ever mentioned it before. On reflection

– namely the bathroom mirror's – it was quite, not exactly alarming, but . . . *intense.*

'Did I mention that I think you're amazing?' Matthew reaches out his hand to brush his wife's arm and then stroke his daughter's dark hair.

Daughter. He turns the word over in his head and takes a deep breath.

'So, what are your plans for today then, Daddy?'

This question throws him. 'What do you mean? I'm going to sit here with my two beautiful girls. What else?'

'All day?'

'Why not?'

'Because if you sit there with that face all day, I will get no sleep, your beautiful daughter will get no sleep and you will die of boredom.'

'This isn't boring. This is . . .'

'A *miracle.* I know, honey.'

Now they are both laughing.

Matthew turns to glance around the room, and then stands and walks over to the bag on the spare chair containing all the baby's things. Soft and impossibly pretty things in white and lemon, because they did not want to know the sex of the child in advance.

They have the privacy of this bright, single room on account of the emergency caesarean. Matthew keeps his face turned away from his wife as he thinks again of the awfulness of it all. Eight hours of the torture they call labour, and then the horror of being told that the child was both in the wrong position and in distress and that a caesarean was essential. It was not at all what Sal had wanted, and he will never forget the look of fear and distress and shock on his wife's face as they wheeled her along to the operating theatre, Matthew clutching her hand and trying to reassure her.

It is probably the reason for this sheer elation. This worship face. The overwhelming tidal wave of relief.

'Look – my suggestion would be for you to go home now for a few hours. Get a shower and some kip. You can pick up my list of things and come back tonight. My mum's calling back again this afternoon, and to be honest, I'm exhausted, Matthew. I could do with just sleeping.'

He turns and moves to sit alongside her on the bed. 'You sure? Doesn't feel right to leave you yet.'

'You've been here hours and hours, darling.'

'Nothing compared to what you've been through.'

She tightens her lips, and Matthew fancies he sees a glistening in her eyes.

'Scary, wasn't it?'

He just nods, afraid that his voice will crack if he speaks again too soon, coughing just to be sure.

'Look, Matthew. I'm stuck here for days now, which we didn't expect. So how about you work on your case a bit until I'm home.'

'I wasn't thinking about work.' A lie.

His wife tilts her head. She knows him so well.

'OK. Maybe just a little bit. But only because you see everything differently once this happens.'

'What do you mean?'

'Oh, nothing.' He wishes he had not said this out loud; he doesn't want to link his beautiful little girl with work, with the new haunting in his head. Doesn't want his wife to make the link either. But the truth is that he cannot help thinking of so many things differently now. The image of Anna from her Facebook page, used in all the media coverage over the past year. Her mother, Barbara. Ella, too. He is thinking about all of it differently. There is a twist in his stomach and he finds himself swinging his right leg to and fro.

'Well, I think it makes sense for you to get some work done in between visiting me, and then you can pamper me when I'm allowed home.'

Matthew bites his bottom lip. Sal had planned to campaign to be allowed home as soon as possible. He was hoping to wind work right down during the first couple of weeks. But the caesarean and the compulsory stay in hospital have thrown everything out.

'OK. You're right. I'll go home, get your washing done, catch up on some work while I can and come back this evening. If you're absolutely sure?'

'I am absolutely sure.'

He kisses her very tenderly on the mouth, brushing his lips on his daughter's head.

'Amazing, isn't it?'

'A miracle,' she replies, her tone teasing but that glistening in her eyes once again.

Back at the house an hour later, Matthew finds himself pacing around. It's so bizarre to think that very soon they are to be back here. A family. Not just him and Sal but the three of them. He glances around, wondering suddenly if the place is big enough. In the corner is a large wicker basket, containing a few new things, many of which seem entirely alien to him. Something called a baby gym, which requires some kind of construction. Changing mats and the like.

It feels all at once wonderful and, yes, miraculous and absolutely terrifying. Matthew wonders if he is ready – if anyone is ever really ready.

He presses the switch to fire up the espresso machine and flicks through the mail. Nothing significant. He puts it on the kitchen counter and takes out his mobile just as the green light signals the machine is ready.

Placing a porcelain espresso cup under the nozzle, he feels the disconnection that true exhaustion brings. That sense of not quite fitting into the space around him. He presses the button for a double, and with the other hand dials Melanie's number. To his surprise she answers instantly.

'I wondered how long before you'd be onto this. So how did you hear? Bongo drums, or are you psychic as I always suspected?' Melanie's voice is hushed.

Matthew feels the depth of his frown and pauses. He hasn't the foggiest what she's on about.

'News travels fast.'

'Does Ella know? Is that it?'

Matthew does not answer.

'Well, don't you share it with anyone because the proverbial is really hitting the fan now. As far as I know the media haven't cottoned on and that's how we want to keep it. For now, at least.'

Matthew stares at the promising crema on the top of his espresso, surprised that the bluff has worked. He takes a small sip, wondering what the hell could have happened. Until last night, the police teams in London and Cornwall wanted as much media coverage as possible. What is it that the police suddenly don't want the press to know?

'How about you tell me what you can, Melanie, and I share everything I've got. Also – I promise to keep an ear to the ground and tip you off if the media get wind.' Matthew has some good contacts among local journalists, and Melanie knows this.

'Strictly off the record.'

'Oh, come on, Mel. You know me. I may have stuffed up my own career but I'm not going to mess up yours.'

'OK, but not over the phone. How soon can you meet me in Saltash? Usual café.'

'I'll text you.'

'Good. And not a word to anyone. OK?'

'Deal.'

'Oh, and by the way, how is Sally? She's overdue now, isn't she?'

A rush of guilt sweeps through Matthew. For a few minutes, he had actually forgotten. No. Not exactly *forgotten* . . . more switched off. It astonishes him that he could let that happen, and wonders if this is how it is going to be. Work. Home. Entirely split-thinking. Suddenly the image from the hospital is back in front of him, vivid and lovely.

'I'm a dad, Mel. A little girl. I have a beautiful little girl.'

CHAPTER 23

THE FATHER

Henry stares around the police cell and finds himself thinking of Sammy. He hopes that Jenny will take him out for a good stretch of his legs, but then leans forward to put his head in his hands. Poor Jenny. To add *this* to all her misery.

He closes his eyes to the memory of the sheer, unmitigated mess he has made of this. Why, oh why, didn't he just have the guts to pull the trigger?

He has tried lying down on the hard, raised platform that passes as some kind of bed, but it hurts his back. The thin blue plastic mattress does little to shield the severity of the concrete slab. He wonders how long he will be held here. He looks at the door and shudders at the memory of the sound it made as it closed. Like nothing you can quite imagine until you are on the wrong side of it. Henry is not normally claustrophobic, but has never been tested in this way before. He is used to the outdoors. To freedom. To fresh air. He tries to remember what the law says. How long can the police hold someone in this way without charge?

They have taken his shoes and belt, and Henry is conscious suddenly that he is probably more used than most to padding around in his socks. Wellies stored in the boot room. No stomach for slippers. He is conscious also that he must have lost weight these past few days, for his trousers feel loose as he stands and walks over to the door with its horrid little viewing grille.

He thinks of Barbara and her plum slices. Of Anna turning cartwheels on the lawn. Her little gang round, running in and out of the sprinkler. What he needs is a Tardis to go back. Yes. To a completely different version of it all.

Suddenly Henry is filled with both impatience and rage. He has had enough of this. All of this. This place. This *bloody place*.

'Could I speak to someone please?'

No reply.

Henry kicks the door and shouts louder. 'I need to speak to someone.'

A few minutes and there is the sound of the grille cover sliding to one side, and the uniformed officer peers in at him. 'Could you keep it down, please.'

'I want to get in touch with my lawyer.'

'I thought you *hadn't done anything wrong* and *didn't need a lawyer*.' The tone is pure sarcasm.

'Well, I want my lawyer now. I know my rights and I'm not speaking to anyone until I get my lawyer.'

'Okey doke. Duly noted. But we're in charge in here and you'll have to wait.'

Henry holds his stare through the grille. 'I haven't done anything wrong.'

'Course you haven't.'

Two hours pass, forcing Henry to face the humiliation of using the nasty open-plan toilet, praying for no movement of the viewing grille as he does so.

He has insisted on his own lawyer rather than a duty solicitor, which is apparently slowing things down.

When eventually he is given time alone with Adam Benson, who until now has only ever handled property matters and his will, Henry realises the severity of his situation and miscalculation. Adam is upfront about his limited experience handling criminal proceedings. Henry says he wants no one else involved. Adam's advice is simple: *Tell me the truth. Trust me.*

'Is there something you need to tell me, Henry? Because if there is, I would strongly recommend you do that now, so I can get on to some contacts who are better placed to handle your situation.'

The truth?

Henry pictures Anna sitting alongside him in the car. Her ashen face. *You disgust me.*

◆ ◆ ◆

Henry can feel his bottom lip wobbling as he is led into the interview room with Adam already seated inside, opposite the wretched DI from London. The man Henry so despises.

'You can't hold me here. I've done nothing wrong. Nothing illegal.'

'You pointed a shotgun at one of my officers, Mr Ballard. We call that *threatening behaviour.*'

'You broke into my barn. I was startled. I was protecting my property.'

'We broke in after you telephoned us in a very agitated state, Mr Ballard, demanding to speak to DS Melanie Sanders. We broke in to prevent you from doing yourself or others harm. You know that and I know that, so how about we drop this nonsense about trespass. Save us all a lot of time.'

Adam turns his head, wide-eyed, and nods encouragement to Henry.

'I was distressed. It got on top of me. Anna's disappearance.' Henry can hear his heart pounding and tries to calm his expression.

He suddenly very much wants to be home, to say sorry to Barbara and most especially to Jenny for the scene at the barn. All the shouting. The stand-off. Poor Sammy barking furiously outside. *The mess. This whole terrible mess.* He also wants to speak to Melanie Sanders, not this prat from London.

'Why can't I speak to DS Melanie Sanders?' When he phoned from the barn he had said he would speak to her. Only her.

'She's not working at the moment. We told you that when you phoned us . . . Now then. The last time we spoke *formally* . . . before this recent incident . . .' The inspector is staring down at some paperwork. Henry assumes it is the statement from his last interview, the one after the TV appeal. 'You gave us your second version of where you were the night Anna went missing. So the *current* story is that your car was left near the railway station for most of the night because you had a bit too much to drink and decided to sleep in the back.'

'That's right.'

'And that's what you told your wife? The reason you asked her to lie for you?'

'Yes. I was embarrassed to have got so plastered. I didn't think it would look good.'

'But here's my problem, Mr Ballard. We've spoken again to the witnesses who phoned in after our television appeal programme, and they didn't see anyone asleep in the back of the car.'

'Maybe they just didn't see me because I was lying down. Or maybe they saw the car before I walked back to it from the pub.'

'Ah yes – the pub. The Lion's Head. Now, here's my other problem. I'm wondering, you see, why you didn't park in the pub car park. Also – no one at the Lion's Head seems to remember you being in that night.'

'It was busy. The car park and the pub. Packed, actually. Why would they notice me?'

Beneath the desk, Henry can feel his palms all sweaty suddenly, and wipes them on his trousers. He turns to his solicitor who is writing things down, and wonders what the notes are for. He looks across at the black box recording the interview and wonders if they will get a transcript. The problem with lying, he is learning, is that you have to remember the details of the lie. To make them match each time. Each new version is making it more difficult.

'How well do you know your daughter's friend Sarah?' The detective inspector has leaned forward suddenly and is closely monitoring his response.

'I don't know what you mean. She's Anna's best friend. Has been for years. She comes around the house a lot, just as all her friends do. We've always made them welcome.'

'And when did you last see Sarah, Mr Ballard?'

'Excuse me?'

CHAPTER 24

THE FRIEND

Sarah is thinking about singing. One of the key things she quickly found she had in common with Anna – beyond the two-ball obsession of those early days – was singing. They were in the choir at primary school together and loved it. Then, in secondary school, they joined the musical theatre group together.

For a number of years, this hotbed of theatrical ambitions provided a rollercoaster of tears and tantrums, triumph and tragedy for the two girls. During years seven and eight, the camaraderie was for the most part entirely positive. The younger girls all sang together in the chorus. But once auditioning for bigger parts was in the mix, everything became more competitive. As the pool of hormones, longing and insecurities bubbled furiously, Anna and Sarah watched all the subsequent falling-ins and falling-outs with a new awareness.

While Sarah surprised many around her with her burgeoning academic talents, Anna became the better singer. By year ten, the two friends were both obsessed with the notion of becoming musical theatre stars. They each believed this to be perfectly possible and hatched a plan to apply together to study music and drama. They imagined sharing a flat and spending their days singing on a West End stage, ignoring the eye-rolling of Tim and Paul and all the adults in their families. Anna's father was especially dismissive.

I blame The X Factor *for this, Anna.* His mantra, sitting in his socks around the farmhouse dinner table, was that it was one thing to enjoy a school production, but quite another to kid yourself there was a career in it. *Do you know, you two girls, where most musical theatre students end up? Waiting tables and pulling pints. You want to stop all this pipe-dream nonsense and work towards a solid degree. The pair of you. Something that will lead to a job . . .*

Sarah and Anna ignored it all. They huddled up in Anna's bedroom, wrapped in her duvet, and watched DVDs of all their favourite shows back to back. *Cats. Phantom. Starlight Express.*

And then – joy of joys – at the beginning of year eleven, the drama department announced that the new production was to be the girls' favourite musical of all. *Les Misérables.*

Sarah sighs and looks at her watch, her eyes narrowing as she remembers it. That first discussion with Anna about which part to try for. She remembers sitting in Anna's bedroom as they fell silent, each realising with excitement and dread what lay ahead for their friendship.

There was suddenly no place for loyalty or compromise. They were each ready to sacrifice their very soul to play Fantine.

From the off, Sarah knew that Anna was more likely to get the part, but that did not stop her trying. In her own bedroom, she secretly watched Anne Hathaway in the film version over and over and over until she had perfected every nuance, every breath, every tear. To her shame, she began to hope Anna would catch a cold or that her father would ban her from the distraction during their important GCSE year.

But no. On the day of the audition, there they both were – best friends and arch rivals – wishing each other well in public but secretly harbouring new and confusing thoughts. Sarah was ashamed but consumed by the depth of her ambition and jealousy.

By 3 October it was all over. A post on the drama noticeboard confirmed it: Anna would play Fantine. Sarah would be in the chorus with the 'additional responsibility' of understudying Madame Thénardier. The baddie.

Anna's face said everything about the nature of her personality.

You want me to withdraw, Sarah? Honestly – if it means so much to you, I'll withdraw. My dad doesn't want me to do it anyway. I don't want this to be a thing between us.

No, don't be silly. I'm pleased for you.

And then for weeks and months she had to watch it all. The spotlight on Anna. Everyone amazed at her talent. All the boys, who dismissed the musical theatre crowd as *hysterical* suddenly seeing her in this new light, as rehearsals were filmed and shared on Facebook. Even Tim and Paul, who both hated musicals, seemed to become more tolerant, showing an interest in how things were going. Sarah still had a secret crush on Paul, and hated to see his funny comments on Facebook telling Anna how fabulous she looked in the costumes.

It was then that Sarah began her diversion. Not a conscious decision. More an experiment to boost her self-esteem . . . and then a steep and slippery slope. She discovered there were other ways to be popular with the boys. At first she felt powerful. She had her own spotlight. Then, very quickly, the grubby flip side emerged. Some gossip and nastiness on social media. A shared picture. And suddenly everything just ran away from her.

It wasn't long before she was openly being called a slag. An ugly rumour went round that she had given oral sex to two boys on the rugby team at the same party.

Anna, ever loyal, told her to ignore the haters. Sarah wondered if deep down Anna suspected she was going off the rails, but they never discussed it properly. Publicly, Anna simply stood up for her. She said that people made things up because they were jealous of how clever she was. Sarah never told her it was all true.

All of it.

That was when their little gang really started to fall apart. Was it because Tim and Paul heard too much from the other boys? Sarah had never been sure.

And now, checking the train timetable on her phone, she realises how badly she needs to go to Tintley, to discuss all of this with the one person who just might understand.

Lily.

For a whole year, Sarah has convinced herself that Antony and Karl are to blame for whatever has happened to Anna. But new and confused thoughts are bubbling up within her and getting stronger every day.

Because Sarah keeps thinking of her father turning up to watch the school's production of *Les Misérables* out of the blue. How much he went on and on about how stunning Anna was in the show.

And she cannot forget the truth about what happened in London. The truth about what happened in the club. And the text.

The text she has been afraid to tell *anyone* about.

WATCHING ...

8pm

I pick those I watch very carefully.

They need to be special. Sometimes I pick them because I love them and I know how much they need me, and sometimes I pick them because I hate them. I never pick anyone in-between. Why bother if you don't feel strongly?

Right now it is difficult because I have had to stop watching for a little while. It is frustrating. Churns me up – like needing a cigarette.

But somehow you have to stay calm. You have to be much cleverer than the people you watch. You have to keep your face looking just right. Speak in the right tone.

This is also the bit I am very good at.

The right face.

The right tone.

So that you don't know who I'm watching. Or why.

CHAPTER 25

THE WITNESS

Luke got the text late last night. *Emily has lost the baby.* We were up most of the night talking, going around and around in circles.

Luke is so shaken – sadness and relief and terrible guilt all mixed up together. She won't speak to him on the phone. He got through once but she just cried, and texted him asking to leave her alone. She doesn't know how to feel. No one does.

I have never seen Luke this low. This sad. I am still keeping him off school. He is getting worried about how much he has missed, but I take the view he can either catch up or sit the year again if necessary. I very much want to stay around to support him today, but I have a dilemma again. I have wedding flowers to finish for a delivery van arriving at 8 a.m. The bouquets need to be at the bride's house by 10.30 a.m. latest, and the rest of the flowers at the reception venue soon after. I have tried phoning a couple of friends in the trade to see if they can take over the order as an emergency favour, but no one is free.

So what can I do? Let a bride down?

Tony is away for two nights meeting other area managers – one of those team-building specials. He couldn't get out of it, as the MD might be there. So I have to make the call. Is it wise to leave Luke, and is it safe to be in the shop early on my own now that the new security is in place?

We've had new locks and an alarm installed, but the blessed system has been malfunctioning and the families that live over the row of shops have been complaining. Something is accidentally tripping it. I've had three false call-outs so far, and quite frankly, I'm sick of it. The system cost us a lot of money and it isn't good enough. The installer keeps making excuses on the phone, implying it is something to do with the way I set it. But I am not stupid, and I have followed the instructions absolutely to the letter.

The last email blabbered on about the system needing time to settle down, as if it was a perm that needs a few days to drop. We're talking electronics. Science. I gave it to him with both barrels, threatened to call Trading Standards. The return email said that mice can set off the alarms. *Mice?* Can you believe it?

I had to go out to the shop at two o' clock this morning, leaving poor Luke for a bit. So here's the confession. Instead of resetting it, I switched the stupid thing off. I know. But it's making things worse, not better. Waste of space.

It is 5 a.m. now, and I need to leave immediately if I am to get these flowers done in time for the delivery van. I make two cups of tea and take one up to Luke's room.

He is sitting up in bed, still dressed in yesterday's tracksuit.

'I made tea.'

He looks at me as if I am speaking another language. As if he doesn't recognise me.

'Do you think everyone in school will find out?'

'I don't know, love. I hope not.'

'Me too. I couldn't bear that. For Emily, I mean.' He puts his head in his hands.

'Look, love. I don't expect you to come to the shop with me. But your dad – he's going to be cross if he finds out I've gone in on my own again, so best we not tell him.'

Luke turns towards me with a strange blank look in his eyes.

'Is it safe for you to go in alone?'

'Yeah. Of course. Don't worry about it, love. We've got the alarm. It's perfectly OK. The police are sure the postcards were just from some attention-seeker. Nasty but harmless.'

'You sure? You want me to come?'

'No, love. You look terrible. I want you to rest and promise me you'll stay safe and, well, to remember that this is all going to be OK in the end. We are here for you. And I know it feels really sad and confusing right now, but it will get better.'

'Are you still worried . . . about that girl? About Anna?'

'No, love. I've tried to stop thinking about it. I'm worried about you now.'

I tell him then that I will be on my mobile and he is to ring or text immediately if there is any kind of worry. I won't open the shop today. Once the wedding flowers are in the van, I'll put the closed sign on the door and come straight home.

'Is that OK, Luke? Will you be OK for a few hours?'

He nods.

'Keep your phone on, love.'

Another nod.

There is never any traffic this time of the morning, and very soon I am sitting in the car outside the shop. Ridiculous, but I have started travelling with the door locks on. I haven't told Tony this, and I don't know what I am expecting to happen.

The truth is I keep getting this feeling at the shop that I am being watched. You know – that odd physical sensation, as if someone has ever so gently tapped you on the shoulder before you turn round to find there is no one there. I expect it's paranoia. I'm not as convinced by the police's reassurances as I've told Luke and Tony I am. I keep thinking about those secateurs.

I have thought about phoning Matthew again, but he has been out of the loop since his wife went into labour and I don't want to trouble him. In any case, he is a private investigator, not a security guard.

I look around the car. No one seems to be stirring. The lights in the flats above the shops are still off. There are probably no more than a dozen to twenty paces between the car and the shop. I have done it a million times, day in and day out. I can't let myself be like this.

Get a grip, Ella.

I take a deep breath, press the lever for the door locks, and get out of the car as quickly as I can. Shop keys already in my hand, I wait until I am in the doorway before turning to fire the key to lock the car. Heart still pounding, I am very soon inside the shop, making sure the door is pushed tightly so that the Yale lock connects. It is a special new lock that needs a key once it is closed, a bit like a hotel bedroom door. During the day, I keep it open with a flower bucket filled with daily specials. For now, I double-check it is fully closed and secure. Good. I leave the blind on the inside of the door down. You can see in through the window display, but that can't be helped. I will be working out the back mostly, anyway.

I move quickly through to my prep area, taking off my coat and hurling it onto a chair while flicking the switch on the coffee machine. I am an order bunny. Last night I loaded the coffee machine ready for this morning while I was doing the six matching table displays which are sitting on the middle shelf of the flower cooler. The blooms for the three wedding bouquets are all carefully set out in water on the bottom shelf, in the order I will make them up. The two bridesmaids' bouquets first, and then the bride's.

When I first started my business, I used to do all wedding flowers the day before. I was worried about running out of time and making a mistake. Now I know exactly how long everything takes and have more confidence. I prefer everything to be super fresh, so I only do bridal bouquets the day before if there are delivery issues or exceptional problems with flower selection.

I used to do the deliveries myself, too, but now I have an excellent guy helping me. Tom is cheap and reliable, he handles the flowers carefully, and he has never let me down. He'll be here in less than three hours, so I need to get cracking.

Today's order is for three informal bouquets with roses and large daisies – flowers that are easy to source. Informal hand-tied arrangements are my forte, but this bride wants traditional binding with ribbon. The bouquets don't take long, but I always build in spare time and I know I will be fine if I get going.

I love that the bride has gone for simplicity. Her dress has a lot of lace so she is sticking with very simple flowers for the contrast. Very wise.

Hot pink gerberas mixed with some tight rose buds for the two bridesmaids. I set everything ready at my workbench, cutting off strips of sticky floral tape and attaching them to the edge of the counter. Next I begin the first bouquet, selecting the best single flower as the centrepiece, and working outwards in a spiral to build up the arrangement. It goes well. The flowers are terrific quality and I am in a good rhythm. This doesn't always happen. Very soon I have the required shape and move over to the mirror that is set up specially so that I can check how the bouquet looks held in front of me. Good. Yes. I am really pleased. Excellent shape. I return to the workbench and use the tape to secure the stems: not too tight, you need to be careful not to damage them. Then I pop this first arrangement back in one of the vases ready on the workbench, glancing across to see that the coffee is ready. I pour a large mug, adding milk from my mini-fridge, and sit down.

It's only now, as I stop thinking of the flowers, that my mind wanders. The hook on the ceiling catches my eye – it's the one we used for Luke's bouncer when he was little, and I picture him bouncing and smiling. So happy.

I tried so hard to comfort him last night, but I just couldn't find the right words. And now I think of how close I came to being a grandmother and it is too much. Tears. No sound: just the sensation of wetness on my cheeks. I let myself cry while drinking my coffee, the saltiness of the tears running into my mouth and mixing with the drink, and then I shake my head and reach for tissues from my bag on the counter. I wipe my face, sniff and turn to look back at the flowers.

Automatic pilot again. I dry my hands carefully on the towel by the sink and select double-sided ivory ribbon from the drawer – the expensive roll set aside for weddings – and the little packet of pearl pins. This bit needs real care.

I lift the flowers from the vase and use my favourite red-handled secateurs to trim the stems to an even length. Then I very carefully spiral the ribbon to cover the stems, turning back the end of the ribbon to make it neat, securing with the pins. I hold the arrangement at waist height to ensure it feels comfortable and check it again in the mirror, then I run my fingers up and down the ribbon to ensure there are no protruding pin edges. All good. It looks beautiful.

The next part is a little more challenging, as I need to make sure the second bridesmaid's bouquet matches exactly so there is no variation or imbalance to skew the wedding photographs. These are the things you learn with experience. How crucial attention to detail is.

I am just glancing at the clock above my sink when I hear it. I keep very, very still, frowning as the noise makes no sense. It sounds exactly like a key in the door.

From where I am standing, it is not possible to see around through the opening into the main shop.

'Luke, is that you?'

No one else has a key.

Again, I keep very still, as if this will somehow negate my presence. Stop something bad from happening.

'Luke – you're scaring me. You all right, love?'

Again, no answer, and so quietly I reach for my bag, take out my mobile and dial for the police.

'Whoever's there, I'm phoning the police. You hear me?'

There is another sound, the door handle being rattled and then footsteps. I move to the doorway so that I can see through to the shop-front, where there is the glare of headlights outside. A car apparently reversing and then pulling quickly away.

Heart beating and my mobile still in my hand, I hear the emergency call connecting at last, just as I see it . . . through the glass. On the floor, just outside the door.

'Police, fire or ambulance. Which emergency service do you require?'

I stare at the object on the ground, less than two feet beyond the door, and a tumble of confused images is suddenly whirring around my brain. None of the pictures make any sense to me.

'I'm so sorry. I dialled by mistake.' I hang up and walk over to the door. I unlock it, step outside and pick the object up, and then quickly lock the door again from the inside.

I press my other hand tight against my chest, willing my heartbeat to slow down as the questions boom in my head.

I hold the object in my hand and stare at it, as if this may somehow change what it is. I turn it over, incredulous at the familiarity of it. All the memories it so vividly stirs.

Then I dial Luke's number.

It rings five, six times before he answers, his voice groggy. 'What is it, Mum? I was asleep.'

'You at home still?'

'Yeah. Course.'

It makes no sense. Why would he lie to me? Why would he want to come down here and scare me?

I stare at the solid piece of plastic in my hand, stroking its outline with my thumb. I know that it is Luke's. And I try to work out what on earth I am going to do now.

CHAPTER 26

THE FATHER

Henry stares at the fly on the wall. He has no idea why the police are asking questions about Sarah. They won't explain.

He has been locked up for what feels like hours and the fly is driving him nuts. For a moment it is still and then it jumps – first diagonally about two feet, and next a second hop vertically. Henry narrows his eyes and tries to process the odd familiarity of this scene, searching his brain until the connection finally dawns.

He laughs out loud. *Norman Bates.* He laughs again, shaking his head at the surreal absurdity. The acoustics in the police cell are bright, and he listens for the echo of his laugh to fade, first externally and then inside his head. He waits for absolute silence, leaning forward to place his head in his hands momentarily before making a decision and standing up.

OK, Norman, so how about this time we kill the fly.

Heartened suddenly by this new resolve – the notion at last of something to actually *do* – Henry glances around the room to answer the next challenge: namely, what he might use as a weapon. For a moment, he considers removing his shirt and flicking it at the fly, but he imagines the custody sergeant peering through the viewing window why so many police officers struggle to balance work and home: both so important but both so full on, so emotionally intense. And he realises, too, that he was right – he will never get to do the psychology degree now. He thinks of the tiny bundle in the pink babygro, eyes drowsy but still searching for her mother.

Everything is so very different now. Life suddenly has different priorities. Yes – a different lens.

CHAPTER 35

THE WITNESS

I am glad that Tony is coming home. Luke was right. I need him.

The problem is I feel so churned up, my head racing with so many thoughts. I wonder what is real now and what is paranoia. It is as if this whole past year has overloaded my system and I can no longer think straight.

Am I so stressed now that I am imagining things? The noises at the shop. Being sure I am being watched. That someone actually came in and moved the secateurs. Dropped the map-viewer outside. Did I imagine it all? Am I conjuring these things?

I don't want to believe Luke is capable of wanting to frighten me, however upset or neglected he might feel. It can't be that. So – what?

I am in the comfort of the sitting room, watching it all on the big television. No. Comfort is the wrong word. Nothing feels comfortable anymore. Even in bed at night, I just can't keep still, taking hours to drift off to sleep.

I have taken the maximum paracetamol dose today but they don't seem to be working. My head is still pounding.

Luke is upstairs, and pops down once in a while to offer a drink, probably prompted by his father by text, in the same way he's reminded of Mother's Day and my birthday. Every time he appears again at the door, I examine his expression closely, wondering if I should just ask him outright. Challenge him and get this sorted. Tell him that I won't be cross but that I need to know. *Have you been more upset with me than you're letting on? Over the sadness with Emily? Over my preoccupation with this Anna case? Did you come to the shop for some reason I can't work out?*

I look over at the bookcase alongside the media unit that holds the telly and the DVD player. On the top are favourite pictures. Luke as a baby. First day at school. Receiving his medal for his first Ten Tors. God, I was so proud that day. The schools make out it is a standard thing in Devon and Cornwall: to take on the 'ten tors', a walking challenge on Dartmoor, as if it is no big deal. A rite of passage for living in such a beautiful place. But the reality, to be frank, is a shock. I wouldn't want to do it in a month of Sundays, and I was surprised that Luke was so keen.

He likes basketball but is otherwise not someone you would describe as especially sporty. Never did the Scouts or anything like that. More into his music, really.

For the Ten Tors challenge, they have to walk in teams of six – with no adult supervision – and they have to carry all their own kit to camp overnight on Dartmoor. The routes are a minimum of thirty-five miles, to be completed in two days, and the terrain is dangerous if the weather goes pear-shaped. Which it very often does.

The army supervises the whole thing, and there are checkpoints at each of the ten tors to prove they have completed the route. But in between that contact, the young teams are entirely on their own. And things can – and do – go wrong.

Once a girl drowned during a training exercise. It was so shocking and there was a big review. I thought, maybe even secretly hoped, they might scrap the whole thing, but no. They just have very strict guidelines.

Schools right across the south-west take part and it gets seriously competitive. Grammar schools versus comps. Private schools versus state. Good-humoured but serious nonetheless. Every team hopes to come in first. Fastest.

The training programme stretches months, as the teenagers have to build up their stamina and skill set. Map-reading. Fitness. Camping. They have to carry tents and cooking equipment and sterilise their own water, too. Loads of kids drop out. But not our Luke. He really surprised us – not only did he stick at it, but in the end he was made team leader. And that first expedition went so well that he went back for more. He did the thirty-five-mile trek that first year, and the tougher forty-five-mile challenge last year.

So – yes. I was prouder than I can ever explain when he stepped up for that photograph to get his first medal. Hundreds and hundreds of teenagers milling everywhere, but I remember hearing his name over the tannoy and taking in that beam of pride on his face as he caught my eye. Right there in the centre of it all. His moment.

And now? Emily has ended their relationship and Luke feels terrible. So up and down. He was so different – so carefree – in that photograph, out there on Dartmoor.

The news from Spain has been going round and round in circles for hours and it is doing my head in. All the major channels have pulled back on the coverage as it is getting repetitive.

I keep thinking of the Ballards in Cornwall. What must this be like for them?

And there it is again. That knot deep within my stomach. Because this really is it. The reckoning. No escaping the fact that I was right to feel guilty. That Karl or Antony or both of them took that girl and did God knows what, all because I made the wrong decision. Because I made a snap judgement. Because I got on my high horse over Sarah's behaviour.

I can feel my lip trembling but I chastise myself. *No, Ella. This is not about you; this is about Anna.* This is about facing up to it all now.

The only mystery that remains: the postcards. The noises at the shop. Who has been rubbing my nose in it? The postcards cannot be from Karl or Antony if they've been abroad all this time. So if it's not Mrs Ballard – who?

The key in the door at last . . .

I wait for the sound of the door clicking closed. The clumping of the overnight case. And to my dismay, it is a trigger. By the time he is in the doorway, I am openly sobbing.

'Oh my God, Ella. It's all right, love, I'm here now.'

His arms around me. My Tony. And I am all at once grateful for those arms and yet guilty also because I still haven't been one hundred per cent straight with him.

'There, there, love. Come on now.'

'It's all right. I'm sorry.'

'Don't be sorry.'

And then, after I finally get a grip, the truth pours out of me. Every single little detail this time. About hiring Matthew secretly to warn off Mrs Ballard when I thought the postcards were from her. About going to Cornwall, against Tony's advice, and upsetting her. About thinking that someone was watching me at the shop but not being sure if I am simply going mad.

'Right. That's it. How about we just close the shop for a little while? You take a break. We get that rip-off company to come back to check the alarms. And you listen to me . . .' Tony has his hands on the top of my arms, leaning in to make me look right into his face. 'This is awful. What's going on in Spain, I mean, and God knows how it's going to turn out. I've been listening on the radio and Anna's parents must be going through hell. But you didn't do this, Ella. This madman Karl is doing this. Not you.'

I don't reply. And now Luke is in the doorway. He looks pale and is shifting from one foot to the other. 'Really glad you're back, Dad. And I'm really sorry I didn't come into work with you, Mum.'

'Please tell me you didn't go in on your own?' Tony grips my arms a little tighter, his eyes wide.

There is a long pause.

'Totally my bad, Dad. I've been so exhausted, so upset. But I've just put out some more feelers on Facebook to see if I can find someone to take over the job.'

'You haven't shared our personal stuff on Facebook, Luke?'

'No. No. Course not. I've just said I know of a great part-time job. I'll vet the responses. If anyone good replies, I'll pass them on to you to see what you think.'

'Well, that's good, Luke. Thank you. I expect your mum would rather pick her own staff, but put out feelers, by all means. So long as you don't share Mum's personal information. But I really don't want your mother there early on her own, meantime. Not until we know for sure how all this is going to turn out.'

'But it can't be the guy on the train, Dad. The person sending the postcards. Not if he's been in Spain all this time.'

'Could be the other guy from the train. Or some random nutter. Please, Ella. Just do as I ask from here on, will you? Yes?' Tony loosens his hold and leans forward to kiss me on the forehead and to wrap his arms around me.

Luke then disappears to make more coffee, and I know exactly what is going to come next from Tony. Sure enough, he is absolutely horrified that I have involved a private detective without telling him. He tries very hard not to sound angry but the disappointment on his face kills me.

'I thought you had told me everything.'

'I'm sorry. I honestly thought I could spare you and sort it all out myself without worrying you, Tony. With everything you've got on. Luke. This promotion.'

'Never mind what I've got on, I just can't believe you wouldn't *tell* me. And going to Cornwall? I told you that was a bad idea.'

'I know. And I guessed you would be cross and I just kept digging, I suppose. Trying to resolve it on my own. I do see now it was stupid to keep it from you. I'm so sorry, love. But I was honestly so sure it was Mrs Ballard to start with, and I didn't want to make it worse for her, to get her into trouble by going to the police.' I then tell Tony everything else. That Matthew has been liaising with a contact in the force in Cornwall. It is such a huge relief not to be keeping this to myself anymore, especially as Matthew has suggested we meet after his hospital visit so that he can update me. Now I won't have to lie to Tony.

Sure enough, Tony says he wants to meet him ASAP. To put him straight.

'What do you mean?'

'I don't think it's right to be liaising with someone outside the force right now.'

'OK. But you might feel differently when you meet him. He's a nice man. Ex-copper and very experienced. He was the one who insisted I give the postcards to the police.'

Tony is about to reply when the news presenter announces they are returning to the scene in Spain for a new development. We both turn to the television screen to see the reporter still standing by the police cordon, with her hand up to her ear as if struggling to hear the link from the studio, and then there is a cut to a really shocking image. Full frame.

It is a grainy photograph, as if taken from a distance, but there is no mistaking it. A tall man at the window of a second-floor flat, with a blonde woman.

A gun to her head.

CHAPTER 36

THE FATHER

Henry Ballard was brought up by the kind of parents who believe children bounce. No cotton wool. No fussing. *Best way to teach a child to swim is to throw 'em in the deep end.* His father's favourite saying.

It was this extreme faith in the innate resilience of children which saw Henry quite literally *bouncing* on bales of hay in the trailer behind his dad's tractor at the age of four, and learning to drive the tractor himself when he was barely twelve.

Looking back now on pictures of his childhood, Henry realises he was lucky not to be on a child protection list. Lines were definitely crossed. And yet? Somehow he and his two sisters not only *bounced*, but thrived. Apart from a broken leg at the age of eight when a cow kicked back as she left the dairy shed, Henry escaped largely unscathed.

And so, emboldened by a general horror of a 'nanny state', Henry approached parenthood himself with a similar, laid-back confidence. *They will be fine*, he heard himself saying over and over to Barbara as she fussed and fretted over high-factor sun creams and anecdotal evidence about skin cancer risks for 'outside workers', as their two daughters ran outside every summer morning, coming indoors only for refuelling.

Farms are dangerous places, Henry, Barbara would say in return while Henry tut-tutted.

You watch too many documentaries, Barbara.

And then little Anna turned five and contracted pneumonia. It started as a standard cough, which Barbara reckoned came from playing in damp hay stored in a side barn, but Henry said she was making too much of it. *She'll be fine.*

Only she wasn't.

The drama peaked with five days in the high dependency unit of the local hospital, including a twenty-four-hour 'touch and go' period when, disconcertingly, none of the doctors would look the Ballards in the eye.

Anna, linked by all manner of tubes to bleeping machines, looked unbearably frail as the little screen kept ringing its alarm bell to confirm that her oxygen saturation levels were very poor. The doctors explained each new strategy, including a drug that could make her heart rate race temporarily but would apparently help her lungs.

One step at a time, the consultant said. *We fix the lungs, then we sort the heart rate.*

Henry is sitting in the lounge now, watching the news as he remembers so vividly sitting in the hospital alongside Anna's bed, racked with guilt as he watched the figures on those monitors. Feeling helpless. Feeling sorry. Sometimes praying to God but then remembering that he wasn't really a believer. Had nowhere to turn. No longer confident in the resilience of children. No longer laid-back. Carefree.

And now no longer the same man at all after his daughter, his beautiful Anna, sat beside him in the car that day he drove her to the railway station to catch the train to London. *You disgust me, Dad.*

Cathy appears at the door, with a large tray sporting their bright red teapot, a jug of milk and mugs. And then, just as she places it on the coffee table in the middle of the room, someone changes the channel again and there is an icicle through Henry's heart.

The picture at the window. A man – presumably Karl – with the gun to the head of his hostage.

Henry hears a strange sound escape from his own mouth, followed immediately by a much louder, horrific wail from his wife. A sound like that of a wounded animal, followed by fast and almost incoherent babbling.

'Oh my God. Oh my God. My poor baby. Henry. Henry – look. Oh no, oh no, oh no . . . We need to do something. Oh my God, tell me what we should do.'

She is standing. Then sitting. Then rocking. Then crying. And then standing again and pacing as she talks . . .

'We need to go there. I need to be there. Henry. Oh my God, I can't be here. I can't be in this room.'

The presenter is saying that the photograph, as yet unverified, is being circulated by a European news agency; that the man has now been clearly identified as Karl Preston but there is yet to be official confirmation that his hostage is Anna Ballard.

'They shouldn't be showing this.' Cathy is taking out her phone and strides towards the hall while Henry moves forward to try to console his wife.

'It's going to be all right, Barbara.'

'How can you say that? How can you say that? We need to go, Henry. We need to go to Spain. We can't be here. I can't be here.'

By this time, Tim is trying to soothe Jenny, who is also crying. Henry catches Tim's eye – the young man also in a state of apparent shock.

'We can't just go to Spain, love. Not yet. We need to be in touch with what's happening.' Henry glances about him. He is thinking that if they are on a plane, they won't be able to follow the news. He looks finally towards the door, realising that he needs the opinion of the family liaison officer, but she is on the phone still in the hallway.

'I could take Jenny to Spain if you like. Wait for you there?' Tim is leaning forward, staring into Henry's face. 'Would that help? To at least have someone from the family there?'

Henry runs one hand through his hair, his other arm around his wife's shoulders as she is sitting back down in the chair now, her head in her hands.

'I don't know. I don't know. Let's see what Cathy thinks. This is all happening so fast. I don't know what they will advise. No, no. I don't think I like the idea of Jenny not being with *us*.'

And then Cathy is standing in the doorway, her face pale. Henry realises there must be more news, but her expression is not good and for a moment he is too afraid to ask what exactly the new information might be.

WATCHING . . .

Friday

Now everyone is looking at her and I do not like it.

I do not like it at all.

It is my job. Supposed to be me. Because I really understand, you see. I am the only one who knows how to watch over her properly. To keep her safe. To understand her. The only one who sees who she really is. How very, very special she is.

When I see other people watching her, looking at her, smiling at her, I get this noise in my head. It is like a clicking at first. Quiet clicking. And then it gets louder and louder until it sounds like thunder all around my brain. And then it thunders around the room and the sky and right out into space.

It's doing that right now. Getting louder and I don't know what to do.

I just need space to think. I need the noise in my head to stop and I need all of these people to . . . stop looking at her.

CHAPTER 37

THE PRIVATE INVESTIGATOR

Matthew feels a yawn break as he reaches for the wiper switch. Mild drizzle – the most annoying kind, especially as he keeps forgetting to change the wiper blades. The soft spray of mist is just too much for the intermittent setting, but not wet enough for the full setting. He tries the washer spray. Empty. Hears his own sigh at the squeak of protest from the screen as he switches between the two wiper speed options. Too dry. Too wet. Too dry . . .

The radio news presenter is on the sport. Matthew checks his watch. There will be a summary of the headlines soon. Good. Bound to include the latest from Spain. Melanie has said he can phone again in case she gets an update from the family liaison officer. She is still fuming over being officially reported by the DI, which is why she is going so off-piste now. Also, she trusts Matthew; she knows he won't let her down.

He thinks of Anna, takes a long slow breath. He has a bad feeling.

He looks at the clouds. Drifting fast in the strong wind. And now he feels the paradox of a smile emerging on his face as he thinks next of his daughter in her silly pink hat in the hospital cot. Her temperature is apparently down a bit – nothing to worry about, the nurses say. Just a good idea to pop her under a lamp until she learns to regulate her body temperature a little better. As he left, Sally was settling down for a doze and little Amelie was snuggled up in her crazy pink headgear to keep her cosy under her lamp. Very sweet. Very funny.

Amelie. Amelie. Amelie.

Mine, he thinks. *Both mine* . . . It still feels so surreal. A family.

But – wait. The jingle for the headlines. Matthew turns up the volume so he can hear better over the annoying grind of the wipers. The presenter summarises what he already knows – *come on, come on, we know all this* – and at last links to a reporter on the scene who is interviewing a police spokesman. Some controversy over new pictures circulating on social media. The spokesman, with a strong Spanish accent, is saying that this is very unhelpful. That the police team are building a rapport with the hostage-taker and this is damaging. Dangerous. Irresponsible. The reporter is saying that it must surely be impossible these days to control things, what with social media. Next, the spokesman is agitated. Says he has to end the interview to take a phone call but is urging people to please be sensible. Not to share these pictures. Please.

The news moves on to another story. Matthew checks his watch again and looks at the bag of washing on the passenger seat. He has agreed to pop in to see Ella and meet her husband, but he does not want to stay long; he needs to get home and get these chores done for Sally. Amazing how many babygros and bibs and bits and bobs a tiny baby can work through in twenty-four hours. There is also a list of things his wife needs. Lip salve. Tissues. Some kind of body lotion – he's forgotten the name already and is glad she wrote it down.

Matthew tries a few different radio channels. *What pictures?* What the hell is going on in Spain now? He finds himself imagining the team briefings behind the scenes. He feels the familiar pull. The sense of loss. Regret. Remembers sitting alone in his new office soon after leaving the force, so desperately missing the sense of being part of something. Something really important.

So how are you adjusting? Sally asked him back then, night after night. He always lied. *Fine. I'm fine.*

Matthew left the force because he messed up. He was responsible for the death of a boy of just twelve. His boss begged him to stay, to take time out to reconsider and to go through some counselling. There was an inquest and there was an independent police inquiry. Both exonerated him of all blame but that made no difference to Matthew. He was the one who had to look the mother in the eye at the inquest. He was the one who woke at night sweating.

It had been a Thursday. Raining that night, too. He was called out by a small, independent supermarket sick of shoplifters. A boy had snatched some cigarettes while the manager was serving another customer and then bolted. Matthew happened across the child running down an alleyway not far from the shop. He gave chase.

Oi! You! Stop now . . .

Even as he ran, Matthew was planning to let the child off with a warning. He had done this several times. The lad was fast but short. Just a kid. But Matthew never got the chance to be lenient. The boy panicked and bolted over a fence and down a bank to the railway line.

Matthew shouted for him to stop but the boy ran across. It was a live line.

It was a terrible sight. A terrible smell.

Matthew was badly burned while pulling the child from the live rail.

I should never have chased him, he told Sally. *If I hadn't made him panic, he would be alive. Two packets of cigarettes, Sally. Two sodding packets of cigarettes.*

You were just doing your job. His wife stroked his hair. He always remembers how tenderly she stroked his hair as he talked and talked – all night.

And so Matthew turned his back on his job. Turned his back on supermarkets who wanted him to chase shoplifters, no matter their age. No matter their motive.

He decided to set up his own business, imagining that it would be better to pick and choose who he helped.

The only problem, as Mel so frequently reminds him, is that he is bored. Cut off from the really important cases. Not many people come to a private investigator with important cases. Too often it is missing people, who disappear because they do not want to be found. And wives worried about their husbands playing away.

Matthew fumbles in the glovebox and finds a forgotten chocolate bar. Good. Sugar. He is now remembering the negotiators' course. Being so surprised by the statistics. That the majority of hostage situations are actually resolved without injury. Of course, that was before suicide attacks. Before the new wave of very different crimes.

The team in Spain will hopefully be doing it by the book – old-school, just as Sally guessed. They would be praising Karl for keeping things calm. Keeping Anna safe. *Well done. You are doing great. This won't be forgotten. That you are keeping everyone safe.*

Matthew closes his eyes and wishes it were him. In the police van. On the phone. In charge.

Never use the word 'surrender', they were taught. 'Coming out' was the preferred phrase. *Let's talk about how you can come out safely, Karl. How we can help you out of there safely.*

During one of the seminars, Matthew asked how they were supposed to respond to demands. Didn't hostage-takers always make bonkers demands? A getaway car? A helicopter? And money. What was the official police response to ransom demands?

Never say no, the instructor advised. Just say, *I'll look into that for you, Karl.* Negotiators should always appear to pass requests through other people, so any negativity or delays do not seem to be their fault. *I'm so sorry, Karl. They're telling me that's not possible at the moment. Let's talk about what is possible. How we keep everyone safe. That's going to really count for you. I'm doing my best for you, Karl, I promise.*

Matthew is still about fifteen minutes from Ella's house and can no longer bear the wait. He pulls into a layby. He has to know what all this blessed talk of pictures is about. He pulls out his phone and calls up Twitter. The images are everywhere. Shots from several different angles, of Karl with a gun to the head of a blonde woman, presumably Anna, at the window.

Matthew feels his heart race as he forces himself into that professional gear: the place where you fight the fear and the panic and you switch on your analytical brain. OK. What does this mean? What needs to be done?

He begins to analyse all the pictures as swiftly as he can. What do they really say? What is really going on? The problem is that in all the shots Anna has her back to the window.

Matthew finds maybe half a dozen different photographs taken from slightly different angles, and frowns. Feels his brain burning, sparks flying as involuntarily he makes connections he does not yet understand. In the force, he learned to trust his gut when this happened. To relax and look and wait.

It is a bit like that series of posters – Magic Eye – where you have to stare and relax your eyes until you almost go into a trance to see the three-dimensional image appear. Relax. Trust your natural ability.

He is flicking between all the pictures and doing this same thing. Something is not quite right . . .

He skims through the messages circulating on social media. The comments are meant to be kind but are seriously unhelpful.

OMG is he gonna shoot her?

There are some messages on Twitter from the police, too, in Spanish and in English, asking people not to take and share photographs, but it is clearly making no difference.

Jesus. A shambles. Matthew skims again through the range of pictures, this time searching news-agency coverage. Some seem better quality, taken by a long-range lens, possibly a press photographer? But most look as if they were taken on phones, perhaps from the window of upper-floor flats opposite the block where Karl is holed up. And then he finds a different shot taken from much higher up. Maybe the top floor of a block of flats, looking down at the window from a different, sharper angle. Now, at last, Matthew sees what was troubling him in the other photographs.

He takes out his iPad to call up the same image and to zoom in a bit. Even as he is dialling Melanie's number he is emailing this image to her. She has to make sure the Spanish team have seen this.

Jesus Christ . . . they *need* to see this.

Five rings before Melanie picks up. 'Mel. I'm sending a photograph over right now. Karl at the window with his hostage. You have to get a message through to the Spanish team.'

'Matthew?'

'Sorry. Yes. It's Matt. On my way home from hospital.'

'I don't have the picture yet. What's going on? Remember – I'm persona non grata. Practically on gardening leave . . .'

'I don't think it's Anna, Mel.'

'What?'

'The girl with Karl. The girl he's taken hostage. I'm not convinced it's Anna.'

'But that's crazy . . . Oh, wait. The picture's through. OK, so what am I supposed to be seeing here?'

'Shoulder width. Wrong body shape, Mel. A rectangle, not a pear.'

'What?'

'OK. Right.' Matthew tries to calm his voice; realises this is going to sound as if he has finally lost his marbles. 'Sal – she's obsessed with the body shape stuff. What clothes to buy. Anna is a pear. Not fat, not at all . . . a very slim pear.'

'Jesus Christ, Matt. Have you got baby brain or something?'

'No, listen. This is important. I couldn't give a stuff about this, but one night Sal made me look at all this nonsense in a magazine. So I would stop buying her the wrong clothes as presents. Body shape apparently doesn't change much . . . even if you lose or put on weight. It's about bones. Skeleton. Fixed. Anna, from all the photographs her family shared, is a classic pear. Same as my wife. A slim pear. Tiny waist, slim shoulders and tiny upper body – slightly broader hips. This girl, the girl in the flat with Karl, is a totally different body shape. Straight up, straight down. Zoom in and look. Shoulders same width as her hips. No proper waistline. It only shows up in this photograph from the higher angle.'

There is silence for a while.

'Are you seeing it, Mel? Check back with the file photos of Anna. Please. Compare them. Compare the shoulders.'

Another pause.

'Christ. I think you might be right . . . But there's no way the team's gonna listen to me, blabbering on about body shape. I'm technically off the case until I see the chief and try to talk my way out of my meltdown with DI Halfwit.'

'So how about phoning your mate . . . Cathy? The family liaison officer. I take it she's with them? We need to know fast.'

Matthew can hear Melanie take in a long breath.

'Please, Mel. If I'm right and this isn't Anna, they need to take a whole different approach. Also – if this isn't Anna . . .' A pause. 'Where the hell is she and what's Karl playing at?'

A huff. 'OK. I'll send this pic to Cathy. See if she will very gently sound out the family. But she may point-blank refuse.'

'OK. Look, I'm about to make a house call myself on the case. The witness – Ella? I promise to share anything I have if you'll keep me in the loop. Please.'

'OK. Though I might be looking for a new job myself.'

'Don't say that, Mel. I was banking on you rising through the ranks so I could make a comeback.' Matthew is surprised to hear himself say this out loud for the first time.

'You kidding me?'

'Course I'm kidding.' He isn't. 'OK. Speak to you soon.'

It takes about fifteen minutes to Ella's home, the rain getting heavier so that he wishes he had thought to put a coat in the car. Matthew checks his watch. He needs to crack on if he's going to get home in time to get the chores done and a decent night's kip. According to Ella and all around him, this is soon to be the stuff of dreams. Poor Sally is having trouble breastfeeding and is already talking about switching to formula. Matthew doesn't mind either way, but is picking up hints that he may well be taking a share of the night feeds. He is starting to wonder how on earth people do it. Work when they have newborns . . .

Pulling up onto the drive of the house, behind a large black BMW, Matthew realises that Ella's husband must be home. He checks his phone – no message yet from Melanie, damn – and braces himself for the rain between the car and the porch.

There is no light on in the hall, but after a few moments he can hear an interior door squeak, strained voices, the click of a light and then Ella is opening the door. She looks pale.

'We've been watching it all on the news. Terrible. Have you seen?'

'Yes.'

Matthew stamps his feet on the doormat. To the right there is a bamboo umbrella stand containing two large golfing umbrellas. A briefcase. The husband definitely home then. Matthew takes in that the briefcase is expensive, the leather well kept. A smart men's raincoat on the nearest hook – silk lining.

Ella is babbling about the news coverage. How shocking it is for so many pictures to be circulating on social media. Matthew is just nodding, waiting to size up her husband's attitude.

In the sitting room, the tension is immediate. Tony is introduced, his body language all conflict. Shoulders held tense. He shakes Matthew's hand but is unblinking, then narrows his eyes, making no effort to conceal that he is weighing Matthew up.

'I should have told Tony before. I realise that now. We normally tell each other everything, so I feel very bad indeed.' Ella is looking first at Matthew and then her husband. Ping-pong paranoia. Ella is a very nice woman and Matthew does not like to see her distressed. 'I was just so sure that the postcards were from Mrs Ballard, you see.'

'And what do you think, Mr Hill?'

Matthew meets Tony's stare and takes a deep breath. 'I think it's understandable that you would be worried, perhaps sceptical even, about my involvement. That's why I was happy when Ella suggested this update. I am hoping I can allay any fears.'

'I'm listening.'

'I was in the force myself. I have a lot of experience and I still have good contacts. And between these four walls, strictly not to go any further, I think they are making an unholy mess of the Anna Ballard inquiry and I am increasingly glad to be involved. To help you, Ella – obviously. But also, I hope, to help get to the bottom of this case in any way I can.'

'Well, that's very noble, I'm sure, but my main worry here is my wife's safety. That's what we're paying you for. Not to solve the Anna Ballard case. That's for the police team. So – do you think Ella is in any real danger? These postcards?'

'Tony, please.' Ella continues to glance from one to the other. 'We're all worried sick about Anna. Of course we are, Matthew. Have you seen the photograph with the gun to her head? Do you think they will calm it down? Or use a sniper? What do you think? I feel so terrible. So worried. Just think what poor Mrs Ballard must be—'

Tony puts his arm around his wife's shoulders, kissing her forehead to quieten her, and Matthew watches closely. Tony smooths his wife's hair very tenderly and Matthew reassesses the aggression, no longer minding Tony's disapproval. He would be the same, were it Sal. No – it is good that Tony is protective.

'I've involved a colleague I trust, over the postcards. There is no way to be sure at this stage but it is more likely to be someone random who has latched onto the case. There is no evidence of a real threat as things stand. That said, I prefer caution until we know more and I have advised Ella to take care. Is there anything else to update me on? Anything unusual? Anything worrying you?'

Ella for a moment looks flustered. Fidgets with her hair. 'A couple of times I thought someone was watching the shop early in the morning. But it could just be paranoia. Headlights shining into the shop early. It just unnerved me because I'm jumpy.'

'You didn't tell me this.' Tony's eyes are wide with alarm. 'Right. That's it. No more working early in the shop.' He turns to Matthew. 'Back me up here, please. She just won't listen. We've installed new alarms . . . though it's all a bit shambolic.'

'Did you see anyone, Ella? Watching the shop?'

'No. It was just a feeling really. Probably because I've been so upset over all of this.'

'Well, my advice would be to close the shop for a couple of days while this situation pans out in Spain.' Matthew is staring directly at Tony.

'Hallelujah. My thinking exactly.' Tony takes a deep breath.

'But what about my flower orders?'

'Stuff the orders, Ella. I'll ring the customers and say you're ill. Recommend other shops – just for a couple of days.' Tony seems pleased, instantly happier, and signals the way through to the kitchen where he is more polite, offering coffee which Ella begins to make. The TV news is on in this room, too, and they all glance at it when they hear a newsreader sharing the latest pictures from the flat in Spain.

While Ella is bustling over the coffee grinder and cafetière, Matthew checks his phone. Still no message from Melanie.

As Ella waits for the coffee to stew a while, she turns to Matthew. 'So will they try to shoot him – Karl? Is that what they'll do? I find it so unbearable, just watching and waiting.'

'A negotiator will be trying to talk him down. Persuade him to come out. It's a waiting game. They won't opt for intervention unless they have no choice. If it is Anna, let's remember he has kept her alive for a year.'

'*If* it's Anna? Who the hell could it be if it's not Anna?' Tony's voice is incredulous and Matthew wishes he had not shared this.

CHAPTER 38

THE FRIEND

'You still haven't explained why you feel it's *your* fault, Sarah.' Lily has made sandwiches on a large platter with slices of apple and peach, which she sets on top of the dresser in her room. 'You really need to try to eat something.'

Sarah's stomach is still unsettled. She looks at the platter, so carefully arranged, and then at her sister. The irony of Lily, all bones beneath her baggy disguise.

'I don't know if I can eat. You have some.' Sarah watches her sister closely but Lily shrugs.

'I ate earlier.'

Sarah lets the lie go. She scans Lily's bedroom, at least pleased for this new privacy, fed up with Moon and the others poking their heads around the door and interfering downstairs, but she is sorry to be away from the large television. She flicks between social media and the news updates on her phone but is wishing now she had an iPad so that she could see better. Also a better data package. She has had warning texts that she's at her limit. No money to top it up.

'Would you mind calling it up on your laptop, Lily? The coverage?' Sarah will not call her Saffron. She watches and tries to find a smile as a thank you, as her sister sets up the computer, searching for a rolling news channel.

'OK. But don't dodge the question, Sarah. This Karl is clearly a nutter and I'm so very sorry this is so frightening for you – what's going on in Spain, I mean. But to be perfectly honest, I'm just relieved Dad wasn't involved. And if Anna upped and went off with this guy Karl . . .'

'She didn't up and go off with him.' Sarah lets this hang in the air and feels suddenly exhausted. It is a bit like that feeling when you stand on a bridge and there is this tiny part of you that wants to jump. To join the water. You know that you shouldn't but you can't help the feeling. And you know that there is this really important decision to be made in a split second and it is frightening. The consequence. The thin line between one choice and the other. Just like with the bottle and the pills, though she realises now that this did not end it. Solve it. Just made it go on and on and on.

'At least, I don't know if she did. Or if he took her, or spiked her drink or whatever, because the point is I didn't look out for her. We had a bad row, me and Anna. And the truth is I just don't know what the hell happened.' Sarah realises as she listens to her own voice, gabbling suddenly, that she just needs an end to this. However awful and shaming and terrible. And her sister – this shrunken and sad version of the sister she has so missed – is her only hope for a full stop.

Lily sits on the end of her bed, her expression changing. A deep frown, then a sort of twitch of the head.

'You need to tell me, Sarah. Please.' Fidgeting with the bands around her wrist again, which makes Sarah want to cry for her. For them both.

There is a long pause. A deep breath that Sarah realises must be her own. And . . . *jump*.

'We had agreed to stay at the club until about two a.m. and then take a taxi back to the hotel together. I was chatting with Antony to start with and Anna was with Karl. It was OK at first. We felt really grown up. I feel stupid admitting that now, but it's the truth. But then they both sort of lost interest in us. They seemed to know quite a few people. Just wandered off. Pretty much ignored us.' Sarah's voice quietens as she remembers how it felt. How angry she felt. How ashamed and duped at how hard she had tried to make Antony like her on the train . . . How quickly he was off, laughing and flirting with other girls at the club. She had thought when they invited them out that it would be like a double date. She had imagined they would sit, the four of them. Dance. Have fun together. But no . . .

'I always get it so wrong with boys . . . with men, Lily.' She is looking up at her sister now. 'They call me a slag in school.'

'You are not a slag.'

She can feel tears on her cheeks and closes her eyes, not caring. 'I just want people to like me.'

She keeps her eyes closed but can hear the creak of the bed as Lily moves to put her arms around her. 'Shhh. Shhh. Sarah. It's going to be all right.'

She shakes off the comfort. 'No. It's not. Anna came to me at about half past midnight and said that she wanted to go early. She'd had enough. She was tired. Very tipsy. But I was looking for Antony still. I was a bit drunk too, and really cross with him, so I told Anna not to be such a baby. To have another drink and to chill out.' Sarah wipes her cheek with one hand, the salty taste of the tears now on her lips. 'That's why we rowed. She told me she didn't feel safe anymore and I more or less told her to piss off. To make her own way back.'

'And that's when she suggested contacting Dad?'

'Yeah. She said that maybe we should get him to come to the club and see us back to the hotel. But I said she was being pathetic and if she contacted Dad I would never speak to her again.'

'Did you tell the police this?'

'No. *Of course not*. I lied. I said Anna was the one who didn't turn up for the taxi later . . .' Sarah opens her eyes to try to read her sister's judgement. Lily looks shocked, and Sarah remembers the look of shock on Anna's face, too. *Please. I want to go back to the hotel now. I feel a bit too drunk. Please, Sarah, I'm begging you* . . . She is wondering how much worse all their faces will look when they find out what happened on the train. With Antony.

'Later I couldn't find her. So I had to take a taxi on my own. I thought she would be back in our room already. Cross with me. I thought I would have the chance to get sober. Say sorry. But when she didn't come back to the hotel, I was in this incredible panic at first, that maybe she *had* got in contact with Dad.'

'Jeez.'

'I was so confused, Lily. Back then, I didn't even know if I was wrong to think so badly about Dad. Paranoid. But I started to think – what if Anna did phone his hotel and he came to the club? Met her outside or something. Oh, I don't know, just mad worries firing round my brain because of the way he *is*, Lily. But I was too scared to tell the police.' She looks directly into Lily's eyes, whose expression says she understands. 'And then Karl and Antony did a bunk and so I thought it was way more likely to be them. And this finally confirms it. That Karl just took her . . . and God knows what . . .' Sarah is openly sobbing now.

'So it *is* my fault. Either way, I messed up, Lily. I completely let Anna down.'

CHAPTER 39

THE FATHER

'I'm wondering if you should phone the family doctor. Maybe a sedative or something? To help Barbara calm down?' Cathy, the family liaison officer, is stroking Barbara's back as she sits, head between her knees, on a chair at the kitchen table.

Henry is standing, hands on both hips, crippled by his own turbulent and twisted emotions. Fear. Guilt. Shame. *You disgust me.* That awful image on the television, which in the end he had to turn away from. That crazy lunatic with a gun to his daughter's head. All he could think of in that moment was of his own shotgun, which the police have confiscated. Of wanting it back. To point and aim. To shoot him. Karl. Dead. *There. Take that.* In the chest. In the head.

He paces as Cathy soothes his wife and keeps looking up at him for direction.

'I don't want a doctor. I don't want a sedative. I need to know what's happening. Oh my God. My baby . . . my poor baby.' Barbara's voice is rising again and Cathy is shushing her, telling her to breathe calmly. To take long, slow breaths.

'She has sleeping tablets but she doesn't like taking those.' Henry feels his lip trembling as he watches his wife's shoulders heaving with the strain of trying to maintain control.

'I really think you should lie down for a bit, Barbara. Upstairs. We'll bring you any news. As soon as we hear anything at all.' Cathy is still stroking Barbara's back. 'Are you sure you don't want the doctor?'

Barbara looks around the room then, as if not seeing what is in front of her. 'No doctor. I want to be in Anna's room. I'll lie down in Anna's room.' She gets up with an odd and worrying look on her face, trance-like, at this new purpose.

'Get Jenny to go with her.' Cathy is directing this at Henry, her eyes wide with concern. Henry, meantime, is helpless. Pacing. Not quite processing the information. 'Get your daughter to go upstairs. Sit with Barbara. She mustn't be on her own.'

Cathy's mobile is ringing once more, and Henry again feels the shudder that coursed through him when he first saw the picture on the television. Cathy says she must take the call, and so Henry moves back into the sitting room to tell Jenny to go upstairs, please, to help her mother.

Tim stands, clearly wondering what he should do. The television is now muted but the picture is of sports coverage. Henry feels a punch of outrage that the world is moving on already. Less than half an hour since that maniac stood his daughter by the window, gun to her golden hair, and the world has moved on to the football.

'I really think you'd better go, Tim. Sorry. But it's all just too much for us.'

Tim just nods, white and shaken, grabbing his coat from the back of the sofa. Henry hears the click of the front door as Tim leaves at last, then moves back into the kitchen, trying to listen in on Cathy's call. She has gone through to the boot room and closed the door. Infuriating. Her voice is muted by the thick oak door.

Sammy has taken the opportunity to sneak through from the boot room, and sits now at Henry's feet, eyes pleading for permission to stay with him in the kitchen. Henry looks at his dog. The glint of amber in his dark eyes. The loyalty. The concern, picking up the tension in the room. He is remembering the puppy on the front lawn, yapping and bouncing to and fro as Anna completed cartwheel after cartwheel on the grass. *Look, Daddy. I can do three in a row . . .*

Henry moves even closer, leaning right by the boot room door, but it is hopeless; he still cannot hear. Cathy is whispering. The desperation to know what is going on burns in Henry's chest like a tearing of the flesh. He closes his eyes. His breath comes loud and laboured through his nose. Sammy is at his side again, nuzzling his leg. *Can I stay, master?* Henry pats his dog's head and feels something inside him break as the dog's tail begins to wag.

Finally, Henry moves over to the scrubbed pine table, on automatic pilot, sitting in the high-backed farmhouse chair vacated by his wife. Only now does he notice that the blue-checked cushion normally on the chair is lying on the floor, just under the table. For a moment he becomes fixated on the cushion, trying to decide if he should pick it up. For a few seconds this decision feels momentous; too difficult to make. And then he is telling himself how stupid and futile and ridiculous it is to even think about this; how little it matters if all the cushions are on the floor. Every stupid thing in this stupid room on the floor. He glances around, clocking all the china, the plates and the jugs and the bowls, and the paraphernalia on the dresser, thinking for a moment that he would like to sweep his arm across it all. Send it all to the floor, to join the cushion. At last there is the familiar squeak of the boot room door, Sammy standing, tail stilled, wondering if he is going to be exiled.

'That was one of my colleagues.' Cathy walks across the room to stand alongside him.

'News from Spain? From the team? What the hell are they waiting for? Don't they have tear gas or something? When are they going to end this?' Henry is surprised at his tone, which is more leaden than angry, not quite matching the words. His head feels the same and he lets it hang down again, looking back at the cushion, noticing a small stain in the left upper corner. Ketchup probably. Another image that makes him close his eyes. Anna lathering ketchup on a bacon sandwich.

'Nothing more from abroad. No. But there is something . . .' Cathy's tone is unusually hesitant. A pause.

'What now? A ransom?' He has been waiting for this, actually, and opens his eyes. 'Because if he wants money, we can get money. As much as he wants. We can sell the farm.' Henry's mind is suddenly racing, thinking of all the people he might ring. Who might chip in. Lend. Help.

'No. Not a ransom. That's not something the team in Spain would want to countenance, anyway . . .'

Stupid of him. How did he think that would play out? Henry stops all the imaginary calls to friends and banks. The local church. The online appeal for cash. He lets go of the scene in his head. A bag of money for Karl. Anna being released from a car, running towards him. *Daddy* . . .

His mind is exhausted from all the chopping and changing. The runaway ideas. The hopes raised and dashed. The horrible imaginings. From the news. All these blessed pictures on social media. The police aren't going to let Karl go, ransom or no ransom. There is no obvious way to make Anna safe. Nothing he can do. That burning in his chest again. Fists clenched tight, eyes fixed again on the cushion.

'I was wondering if I could ask you to look at a photograph, Mr Ballard.'

Henry notices the formality. Cathy has encouraged them to use her first name. She always calls Barbara by hers. At first she called him

Henry, all tea and sympathy and tilting of the head. But since the barn and the shotgun and the interview, he is Mr Ballard. Will probably stay Mr Ballard from here on – a whisker from suspect status – until this is all resolved.

You disgust me, Dad.

'This photograph, Mr Ballard. It hasn't been shared widely. I should warn you, it's another shot of Karl at the window with the gun. The very upsetting image. The one that was understandably too much for your wife. But it's taken from a different angle. And it would help if you would look at it very carefully for me. If you think you're up to that?'

'Of course I'm up to it.' A lie. Henry braces himself. He does not want to look.

Cathy passes him not her iPhone, but her larger iPad.

'It's a shot taken from the flats opposite. From a higher angle. It's been tidied up a bit and there's a zoom.' She sweeps her finger across the screen to show him the second version.

Henry feels his lip trembling. 'So what am I supposed to say? Supposed to be seeing?' Torture. He doesn't want to look at it. The gun. The hair.

'Karl has refused to let his hostage speak to the negotiator. Also, he hasn't sent a photograph through to the police team, which they have requested several times. It's standard procedure. To calm things down and to reassure that the hostage is OK. It's an exchange process. Bartering. If you send us a photograph or let us speak to the hostage, we will do this . . . Send in food, or another phone, or headache tablets or asthma inhalers or whatever it is he needs.'

The hostage? Why is she saying that? Why isn't she calling her Anna? How dare she. This is his daughter. She should use her name . . .

'What I'm asking is this. From this photograph, how sure can you be, Mr Ballard, that this is definitely Anna?'

And now Henry's head is in a whirl. Is she serious? A maniac on a train talks his daughter into some seedy club after her theatre trip. He gets her drunk and God knows what. He kidnaps her. He takes her to Spain. He holes up in a flat with a gun and . . .

'Please look at the photograph very carefully. Especially the girl's body shape. Her waist. The width of her shoulders in particular. Is that Anna?'

Henry looks at the image, feeling the ache of his frown. Shape? What does she mean – shape? Only in this moment does he realise he has a terrible headache. Maybe a migraine; he has had it for hours now, ever since the police station.

The photograph is grainy, not good quality, especially in the zoomed version. The hair is definitely Anna's.

'I don't understand. Who the hell else could this be?'

'Please. Just look carefully.'

Henry stares at the girl, back to the window with a gun to her head. He finds that he is rocking his body now. He is thinking of Anna facing away from him, looking out of the kitchen window. *Look, Daddy, there's that magpie, back again* . . .

What is he supposed to be seeing in this picture? Body shape? What kind of person asks a father to think about his daughter's body shape?

In this photograph, Anna is wearing a tight jumper. Grey, though that might be distorted by the camera, the picture almost certainly taken on a phone.

Henry looks, as instructed, at the waist. The shoulders.

A jarring. Something not right. Oh my God . . .

'Are you saying she might be pregnant? Is that what you're implying?' Henry is fighting very hard not to lose it. He does not want to lose control in front of this woman. He looks again at the photograph and again feels the jarring. Something he cannot quite understand.

'No. That's not what I mean to imply. Her shape. Shoulders. Waist. We all have a set shape, Mr Ballard – a ratio which doesn't change even when we lose weight or put on weight. Or even pregnancy, though that isn't what I meant at all. Shoulder-to-hip ratio. Does this look like Anna to you?'

And now Henry is holding his breath as the enormity of the question and the consequence is sinking in. 'I think we need to call Jenny down here.'

CHAPTER 40

THE WITNESS

I am relieved that Tony has finally gone upstairs to change.

'He doesn't mean to be like that.' I am staring at Matthew, but my thoughts have followed my husband upstairs, watching him put his suit carrier behind the door. His toiletry bag back in the bathroom. Tired. Sitting on the bed. Worried for me.

'No, don't apologise. It's good that he's protective. I'd be exactly the same if it were my wife, and I'm actually very glad we've met now. It's better. For you, I mean.'

I smile at this as Luke comes into the kitchen, rummaging in the cupboard for the biscuit barrel. I consider stopping him; I really should make something proper to eat, but the strain of everything has thrown me.

'I'm sorry, Matthew. How rude of me – I haven't even asked about the baby and your wife. How are they doing?'

The change in Matthew's face is immediate, that bright and bemused sense of pride and disbelief, the punch-drunk expression of wonderment you carry in those early days. It's touching. 'Great, thank you. Really great. She had a C-section so is a bit fed up and a bit sore. Stuck in hospital for a few days.'

'Tell her to make the most of the rest. This is Luke, by the way. My son. Luke – this is the private investigator. Matthew. Remember I told you?'

I watch closely as Luke eyes Matthew with a wariness to match his father's. I feel defensive of both Tony and Luke suddenly. Matthew is right. It is good that they look out for me. I think of all that Luke has been through these past few weeks with his girlfriend, and feel disloyal and foolish for my suspicions over the stupid map-magnifier. How on earth could I have gotten myself into such a muddle? I will not tell Matthew and I will not challenge Luke. Maybe the wretched thing was in my own pocket somehow. Yes. Maybe *I* was the one who dropped it.

'Are we having supper?' Luke is blanking Matthew and staring at me.

Sometimes I wonder if life would have been easier for Luke with a sibling. Someone to confide in. Nearer his own age. We did try for another child. They never found anything wrong but it just never happened.

'To be honest, I think I'll order something in. Do you fancy Chinese, Luke?'

'Great.'

Once he has left the room, I confide in Matthew just how big a trial it has been for the whole family this past year. My fault. Me not being myself; so preoccupied with this case, especially since my name was leaked. The wretched postcards. Longing for it all to *end*.

'Are you sure there isn't anything else you need to tell me? About someone watching the shop? You didn't notice a car colour? Anyone odd hanging around? At the shop? Or here?'

'No. Just an odd feeling, really. You know – that sensation when you feel someone is watching. Like I say, I've been so jumpy. Probably paranoia because of those stupid postcards.'

'OK. Well, I'm sorry, Ella, but for now I'd better go.' Matthew is checking his watch.

'You'd be welcome to stay. Share the takeaway?' Even as the words slip from my mouth I regret them.

'No. Very kind but I have chores to do. But you know you can call me any time. If anything happens. If anything worries you.'

'Thank you.' I find I am embarrassed by the extremity of my relief that he will not be staying for the meal. It will be so much more relaxing for Tony and Luke. I really must learn to put my family before my blessed manners. I like Matthew, but I have to remember this is his job. I switch the channel on the television so we can just quickly check there is no update from Spain before Matthew leaves. As he reaches into his pocket for his car keys, I hear a text buzz on his phone.

'Is it the case?'

He nods and is reading, his face darkening, before looking up at me.

'OK. So this is in the strictest confidence, Ella. But there is some quite difficult news. I suspect it will be a while before this breaks openly. But I have a contact in touch with the Ballard family and . . . Well. I feel you should know this now.'

I brace myself, muscles taut in my stomach. Also my arms, palms pressed flat into my thighs. I am looking at the television, where the shots of the flat in Spain show that the curtains are now drawn. The scrolling headline along the bottom of the screen says there have been no new developments. But I am afraid that Matthew is going to tell me the worst. The bubble of hope burst.

'Is she dead? Has he killed her?'

'No, Ella. The woman in the flat. The hostage. It isn't Anna. We have no idea what the hell Karl is playing at. But it *isn't* Anna.'

CHAPTER 41

THE FRIEND

Sarah is lying in Lily's bed, staring at her sister asleep on the blow-up mattress alongside. Lily is doing the same sweet thing she did as a small child, the index finger of her right hand pressing the tip of her nose. When they were little, Sarah would tease her.

Why do you do that, Lily? Push your nose up when you sleep?

Helps me breathe better.

That's ridiculous.

I don't care.

The bracelets are still around Lily's wrist, and Sarah is wondering if she at least takes them off in the shower. Moon popped in earlier; Sarah is certain now that they are an item, but she is relieved he has backed off for now. Maybe Lily had a word when Sarah took a bath.

Sarah is exhausted, and though the bath was soothing, she always knew she would struggle to sleep. She wanted to take the mattress on the floor but Lily insisted. Even managed a joke. *I can keep an eye out for monsters under the bed.*

The room is thankfully not in pitch darkness. There is a small pane of glass above the door, letting in gentle light from the landing. Lily explained that a couple of others in the house suffer insomnia and bad dreams, so a gentle light is plugged in on the landing so they don't feel afraid when they have to get up in the night.

Caroline, the woman who owns the house, is apparently returning in the morning and Sarah is nervous. She needs to ask if she can stay a while. She can't bear the thought of returning to her mother, not after all she has learned from Lily. There have been more text messages, pleading for her to come home, but Sarah has been curt with her replies, saying only that she is fine and that she is with Lily. *Leave me be.*

But Sarah is torn – like Lily, she is relieved that her father is not involved in Anna's disappearance and yet it is a temporary relief, not a full stop. They surely have to do *something* about their father. They can't just pretend that the past didn't happen. What if he targets someone else? Won't that become partly their fault if they don't step up?

Sarah can't believe that their mother wouldn't believe or support Lily when she told her. And now she feels her eyes scrunched up tight as she realises she should have spoken up herself – done more to reach out to Lily, rather than blaming her for abandoning the family.

She moves as quietly as possible onto her back and tries to calm her thoughts, to examine the shadows around the room again. In the corner there is a shop dummy made of some kind of bamboo that Lily uses as a clothes stand, draped mostly with scarves and a patchwork poncho. In daylight she had admired it – *very boho* – but in the shadows it looks foreboding, like a headless person, and Sarah has to concentrate hard to pick out and identify all the items individually to make them less ominous. Scarf. Scarf. Poncho. *Just clothes, Sarah.*

And now, uncomfortable already on her back, she moves onto her side to examine the robe on the back of the door. It is so long that it trails on the floor, and Sarah finds herself thinking that they should move the hook higher up on the door. Yes. Just a few inches and the robe won't get stuck under the door when it's opened.

Then it is suddenly all confusion. Sunlight. The swish of curtains. A tinkling of glasses or crockery. Distant voices. By some miracle she has slept. Sarah can't believe it. There is a rattling of china right alongside her, and Lily has a wooden tray with two pretty cups of coffee and a plate of something triangular and ominously green.

'Avocado on toast. No excuses. You really must eat something today, Sarah.'

Sarah yawns and stretches. 'OK. Goodness. I can't believe I finally fell off.' She looks at the tray and reaches for a slice of the toast. 'I will if you will.' She dips her head to signal that Lily should have the other slice.

Her sister narrows her eyes, then takes the piece of toast and sits on the floor, pushing the mattress out of the way.

'I honestly didn't think I would sleep. Last thing I remember it was about three a.m.' Still Sarah's voice is distorted by yawning. 'So do you think Caroline will let me stay a bit? I can look for a job in a café or something.'

'I don't know. But I'll ask. Only for the summer, mind. You need to get cracking with your A levels.'

'Not sure I'll bother now.'

'Please don't say that, Sarah. I'm only asking if you can stay if you promise you'll finish your exams.'

Sarah shrugs. The toast is nice. The surprise of lots of pepper on the avocado. Lemon, too. Popping the final piece into her mouth, she reaches down to the floor to pick up her phone. A string of messages. Sarah sits up, leaning back against the wooden headboard and skims through them.

Oh God . . .

She can't take this in. Not Anna? How the hell can it not be Anna? What kind of new madness is this? There are messages from Jenny, from Tim, from Paul and other friends, too . . .

236

She swipes to a news app and asks Lily to put up the news feed on her laptop again.

'They're saying it's not Anna. The girl in the flat in Spain.'

'What?'

It takes a few minutes before the sound is up on the laptop. Lily and Sarah squeeze together on the edge of the bed, shoulders touching, to hear the reporter outside the flat in Spain confirm that the drama is finally over. Karl is now in custody, being questioned by police.

It's been confirmed that the young woman allegedly being held hostage by Karl is not the missing English girl Anna Ballard. Both Karl and the blonde woman in the flat are unharmed. Police are saying nothing further at the moment.

'Not Anna?' Lily is pale. 'This doesn't make any sense at all.'

Sarah feels her hands come up to her mouth – her index fingers pressing into her lips. She can feel her sister trembling through the touching of their shoulders.

'You know what this means, Lily?'

Her sister leans forward, head in her hands, and Sarah gently rubs her back as Lily begins to cry.

'I'm so sorry, darling. I know it's awful, Lily. I know it's not what you want, but we have no choice now.'

Lily carries on crying, and Sarah has no idea how to comfort her. They both know what they have to do.

They have to go to the police about their father now. They have no choice. Sarah has to tell them everything.

CHAPTER 42

THE FATHER

The next week sees a heatwave. A great sweeping 'high' on every forecast. Henry watches it with a quiet fury. The only time the weather people get it spot on – when you can look out the window and call it yourself. His daughter, meantime, is completely forgotten. No longer the headline. The local news is full instead of temperature charts, with chuffed tourist officers babbling about records being broken and how the staycation is back in fashion. *The best season in years.* All around Devon and Cornwall, faces turn a golden brown to match the grass.

Today there is a news report about dolphins being seen more regularly and in bigger numbers off the coast, and some marine biologist is saying there could be more sharks soon. Global warming.

'Global warming – yeah, right.' Henry is packing some more of his clothes into another suitcase, the TV on quietly in the corner of the bedroom. Every time he returns to the house for more belongings, he drags things out as long as possible, hoping that Barbara's resolve will weaken. That she will make tea. Talk to him. Let him stay. But no. Her voice is now shouting up the stairs. She would like him to hurry up, please. To get his things before Jenny gets home. Their older daughter is out with Tim and Paul, apparently. Barbara says the boys have been her rock since things spiralled so terribly.

And now we are all back in the most appalling limbo, Henry thinks as he zips his case. *Anna is still gone. The news obsessed with the wretched weather. And I am in exile.*

Back downstairs, he tries one more time.

'Can't we at least talk, Barbara? Try again? For Jenny?'

'Try? You have the nerve to ask me to try? After you practically blow your head off in the barn, and then I find out you have been putting it about on our very doorstep. Off with some local whore while our daughter . . .'

Henry still has no idea how Barbara has found out about his fling. She doesn't know who yet, thank God, but she's put the pieces together somehow. He suspects Cathy has deliberately let it slip, though she firmly denies this. Since the Spain debacle, their family liaison officer is no longer with them as much. Just checks in daily for a coffee and a chat. Probably embarrassed about the complete pig's ear the police have made of the whole inquiry.

The Spain 'siege' turned out to be no such thing. They learned that the blonde in the flat with Karl was his new girlfriend. The two of them staged the whole hostage thing to try to negotiate for a getaway car. Made it up as they went along when the police first turned up to arrest Karl after the tip-off.

All the Ballards have been told since is that Karl seems to have an alibi for the night Anna went missing. Antony has turned up on the same building site in Spain, too. Both now in custody. Both denying any involvement whatsoever in Anna's disappearance. Their story is that they lost interest in the two girls within the first hour at the club, and have no idea what happened to them. The lads say they went to a party with friends after the club in Vauxhall, which was always their plan. This new information has been cross-checked with witnesses and CCTV, and so far all the images and statements seem to confirm this story. To date, the Met team have not been able to find any gaps in the timeline that would suggest any involvement in Anna's disappearance.

The two men say they only did a runner early the next morning for fear of being blamed or framed. They believed they would go straight back inside. So mates provided false passports and a boat crossing to France. Forensic teams have checked the flat where the party was held. New alibis are still being grilled. But so far – zilch. Karl's girlfriend, the so-called hostage, is an English waitress he met in a bar six months back.

The Ballards have been assured Karl and Antony will almost certainly be heading back to jail for jumping parole and for Karl's fake siege. But as far as Anna is concerned? The police seem slowly to be dismissing the two men as suspects. And they have no other leads. The DI is back in London, apparently distracted yet again by his serial killer case.

So, what the hell now? Henry keeps asking.

We are continuing enquiries. The case is very much still live . . .

In this heat, Henry is slowly facing his greatest fear. That they will never find their daughter; never find out what happened. To imagine this as his future – all their futures – is unbearable. He sees it in Jenny's eyes, too. And his wife's.

In this terrible limbo, Barbara has finally given in to antidepressants but seems to be suffering severe mood swings as a result. According to Jenny, the problem is that she refuses to take them every day, and the inconsistency in the dose is playing havoc with her system. Henry never knows how he will find her: dull and quiet, with all the light gone out of her eyes; or manic, cleaning the house over and over and shouting at him whenever he tries to reason with her.

'You should see the doctor again, Barbara.'

'It's no longer any of your business what I do, Henry.'

He feels this punch inside. Not just guilt, he finds, but a deep and all-pervading sadness.

'I still love you, Barbara.' As he says this, he realises much too late that it is true, and he wishes he could turn back the clock to dilute his irritation, his dissatisfaction with this life – farmer turned campsite manager.

'Well, lucky old me, eh?'

'I'm not giving up on this family, Barbara. We have to think about Jenny.'

'What family, Henry?' She spits this out at him. 'In case you hadn't noticed, we don't have a family anymore. Anna is gone, and I don't know that we are ever going to get her back. And Tim and Paul are thinking more about Jenny's needs than you ever did.'

'That's not fair.'

'Fair? I'll tell you what's not fair – that you don't even have the guts or the decency to tell me who you were with when our daughter went missing.'

Sammy is standing by Henry's side, and he can feel the tension in the dog's posture. Tail down. Eyes down.

'Oh, just get lost, will you, Henry. And take your dog with you.'

'I'll be in touch.'

'Can't wait.'

Henry wheels the suitcase behind him out to the Land Rover, and pretends it is heavy as he lifts it into the back. The truth is he is taking only a few items of clothing at a time, for the excuse to return, still hoping that Barbara will reconsider. He is finding it hard to believe that this is it.

All gone.

He glances one more time at the front lawn, closes his eyes to that picture of Anna turning cartwheels then sitting and smiling. Waving at him.

He feels his fingers flicker, wanting to wave back at her. Finally he pushes his lips together very, very tightly, opens his eyes and drives along the narrow approach road out to the holiday lets – one of the larger, original barns converted into a row of four units. For now, Henry is using one of the two-beds. It feels like playing at life rather than actually living it, not least because the neighbouring three units are full of holidaymakers, and the yard full of bodyboards, wetsuits, laughter and an awful lot of sand.

Henry takes the suitcase into the sad little bedroom with its neutral walls, neutral bedding and fake oak floor. Barbara spent a lot of time explaining to him during the conversion that 'practicality' was the watchword. Also ROI, which he learned stands for 'return on investment'. The fittings and fixtures needed to be neutral, hard-wearing and easily maintained, she explained. It was not about personal taste or personal choice but about ROI. He stares down at the 'easily maintained' floor and thinks of the richer, original oak floors in the upstairs of the farmhouse. The twists and the knots. The lumps and the bumps.

Henry lies on the bed and stares at the ceiling. He thinks of his preferred world. The real world he still clings to. The hay sorted, thanks to the weather. The lambs weaned and turned out onto the grass. What next? He must decide whether to begin ploughing the upper fields for next year's cereals. Should he even bother? Is all this playing at farming going to continue, even? He looks around the room. The tiny pine wardrobe. The matching chest of drawers and bedside table. All too new. Too orange in tone.

He thinks of Sammy next door in his bed in the 'easily maintained' kitchen, the poor dog as utterly miserable and confused as he is. *What are we doing here, master?* those amber eyes ask every day. He closes his own and wills sleep to come, but there is the screech of the doorbell. Another horribly modern touch. High and shrill, unlike the older bell system at the farmhouse.

Who the hell . . . ?

Henry pauses, hoping they will go away, but the shrill noise is repeated. Then a third time. A fourth. Eventually he gets up to see his visitor peering through the central glass pane in the front door.

'Oh goodness. Jenny. Jenny, come in. Sorry. I didn't realise it would be you.'

His daughter glances around the mess that is his open-plan living. A pile of dirty crockery in the sink because Henry keeps forgetting to buy tablets for the dishwasher. His overalls thrown over the kitchen table and his muddy boot prints across the floor.

She marches across to the fridge and looks inside. She sniffs the out-of-date milk and shakes her head. The only other contents are some pre-packed sandwiches and two multipacks, one of sausage rolls and one of pork pies, bought from the local garage.

'Right. That's it. I can't bear to see you like this. We're going shopping together and then I'm cooking supper. Come on.'

'No, love. You don't need to do this. I said I'm fine.'

'You're not fine. Come on.' She is jangling the keys to her car – a battered Fiesta. Henry bought it for the girls to share. Jenny passed her test first time, and Anna was due to start her driving lessons soon. Henry tries very hard not to think of this. He was actually planning to stretch to a second car down the line, so they could have one each.

An hour later and back from the local supermarket, Henry watches his daughter checking all the cupboards for pots and pans to make a bolognaise.

'I'm being lazy using a jar of sauce but it'll taste all right. Not as good as Mum's, but better than pork pies.'

She is sizzling onion and garlic in a pan, and he watches her brown the meat and add the sauce, ashamed of his own inadequacy and wondering when she learned to cook. He hadn't noticed.

'I expect you think I'm a right old dinosaur. Not being able to cook.'

'Wasn't any need, up until now. Was there?' Jenny looks pale and Henry is wondering what it is she has really come to say. He can sense it. The holding back. They tiptoe around each other while the food cooks, and he doesn't push.

The meal is good and Henry is grateful and guilty all at once.

'I forgot Parmesan, Dad.'

'Never mind. I can't tell you how much I appreciate this. Doesn't feel right at all – you looking after me.'

'So, is it true? You had an affair? Mum won't say much. She just lies in bed a lot of the day now. She's been sleeping in Anna's room. Curled up with her old jumpers.'

'Oh, darling, I'm so, so sorry you're having to deal with this on your own, on top of everything.' Henry takes a deep breath. He cannot look at her. 'OK, I admit it. I was a stupid idiot and I really regret it but it didn't mean anything. I promise you. I love your mum. And you mustn't blame her for being so upset. She has every right.'

'Do you think she will forgive you? Let you home?' There is a wobble to her voice and Henry can hardly bear it. 'It just feels as if everything is gone.'

Henry puts his hand out to take his daughter's. The gesture makes her start to cry, and next she is saying something he cannot understand.

'I've just had this awful message from Sarah, too. She's still with her sister in Devon. And she says . . .' Jenny looks into her father's face, tears dripping unchecked down her own.

'Look – Sarah won't say why. She won't give me any details. But she says we have a right to know that the police in London might be questioning her *father*. Over Anna.'

'Bob? Sarah's dad – Bob?'

'Yes.'

'But why? I don't understand.'

'I don't know either. I mean – they questioned you. Is it that they question all the dads? Is that all it is?'

'I don't know. Bob? But why now? Bob's been gone for years. I got the impression he wasn't even in touch with his family.'

Henry feels the confusion shaping his new expression. The muscles straining with puzzlement. He glances across the floor from spot to spot. His wellingtons. The dog back in his basket. The empty shopping bags. A memory of Sarah and her parents when she was little at the village fair. Sarah and Anna on a ride together, new friends, with the four parents making small talk. Bob – tall and aloof. Handsome. A bit cocky. From the off Henry didn't like him.

And then he remembers something else: how Bob was always taking photographs. Endless photographs of all the children. The family didn't seem to have a lot of money but Bob had this expensive camera with lots of lenses. Proper camera bag. Barbara said it was nice that he wanted the memories but Henry thought it was a bit odd. Was rather glad when Bob left the village.

No. Surely not?

There is a strange new sensation in Henry's stomach.

'I need to phone Melanie Sanders. That nice DS. She's back at work now. She'll tell me what's going on.' Henry is standing to take out his mobile with one hand and raking his fingers through his hair with the other.

'And you need to phone Sarah again. Go on, Jenny. Please. Push her to tell you what's going on. Ring her now.'

But Jenny doesn't move. Just staring at him, tears still dripping from her chin. 'There's something else, Dad.'

WATCHING . . .

Thursday

This is not good. Not good at all.

I don't like this heat. And she doesn't like it, either . . .

I have to think very, very carefully now. Must not let myself get muddled. I'm not good when I get muddled.

Most important of all, I need to stop all these wretched people, thinking that this has something to do with them when it has absolutely nothing to do with them . . .

Is none of their business.

If they had just let us be, it would have been all right. But people are so stupid. So now I have to do something to make it all stop.

No choice.

Their fault, not mine.

No choice . . .

CHAPTER 43

THE WITNESS

So often this past year I have wondered what exactly makes us the way we are. I don't just mean the nature/nurture thing, I mean the sum of our personality and the decisions we make. All the thoughts that fire around our brain, even when we don't want them to. How we handle the issues of conscience and responsibility. Why I blame myself when others wouldn't.

Tony says my biggest problem is that I overthink things, that I take the world on my shoulders, and I just need to relax more and stop going over everything. I sometimes wonder if I would be a different kind of person if I could just learn the trick to do this. To stop with the analysing and concentrate on one thing at a time. But my brain simply doesn't work like that. Never has. I'm always thinking, thinking, thinking. A million things competing all at the same time. Constant and exhausting buzz.

Take today. Like everyone else, I am too hot, but I feel just a little bit embarrassed in short sleeves because my arms are not what they used to be. As I unpack the flowers, I keep getting a glimpse of myself in the mirror set up on the wall to check the bridal bouquets. How they look held at waist height. So that right now I am thinking not just of the

flowers and the heat but of my fat arms – in fact, I have all of the following thoughts at the very same time. That I should put something up
on the blog about how to keep flowers fresh in this weather. Yes. People
like tips. That I need to sort out the flower presses with the stock that
has 'gone over' in the heat, to make up some pretty labels and cards for
the window. That I really don't like the way my arms look in the mirror
here at the back of the shop and I wish I had brought a shirt. That I am
glad Luke reckons he has found a couple of people who could take over
his job. He's going to vet them first, then introduce them to me. Quite
frankly, I would rather handle the whole thing myself, but there's been
no response yet to my sign in the window and I don't like to burst his
bubble. It seems to make him feel better to be helping with a replacement, so I am letting it be.

I am also thinking that I wish Tony didn't have to be away again.
That we need to get someone in to check the boiler at home. That I
need to do a sign for the window, recommending flowers that do well
in this weather.

That it is not my fault after all, about Anna. But it still feels it
somehow. I just can't let it go.

See what I mean? All these thoughts, all at the same time. Small
wonder I get so many headaches.

I have ordered in extra lisianthus and roses this week, as both do
well together and in these hot conditions. They're long-lasting and good
value and very stylish. I must remember to put that on the blog, too.
Personally, I like all white, but the purple lisianthus are gorgeous, so
I've ordered more of both. I'll put most in the cooler, with a few on
display to show how versatile they can be. They look so different in
varying vase heights.

I am trying not to bother Matthew, not least because he is supposed
to be taking a break now that his new family is home, but also because
my part in this whole terrible case is technically over.

I still find it hard to believe. Karl and Antony apparently in the clear over Anna. A complete shock to everyone, me especially. Matthew says this kind of thing happens a lot during big investigations, a sudden and unexpected twist, which is why you always have to keep such an open mind.

Tony, in the meantime, sees it all more simply; he says I now need to just put the whole thing behind me. *You see. Not your fault at all. Never was, Ella.*

The problem is that I still keep thinking about her. Anna. That beautiful picture from her Facebook page, hair blowing back in the wind. Where is she? What happened to her really? I worry now, more than ever, that we may never find out.

Goodness – it's three o'clock already, and with all the urgent work done, I decide to stop this; to pop home to get a light shirt to cover my arms. Silly, I know . . . but we are who we are.

I finally make it home, and as I pull into the drive I notice that the curtains upstairs are still drawn. I must have forgotten them when I left. The garden's surviving surprisingly well in this heat. You get a few people raising their eyebrows when I pop the sprinkler on in the evening, but there's no ban so I don't really see why not. We pay the bill.

The porch door jams a little as I try to open it – a couple of those advertising booklets. I wish they wouldn't leave them. Such a waste of trees. I've registered for that system which is supposed to block junk mail. It's reduced the flow a bit but there's still a lot hand-delivered, which is infuriating.

Inside, I notice Luke has popped the pile of mail on the little bookcase by the front window, and I skim through it. Phone bill. Someone who reckons we might be interested in new windows. *No, thank you.* A letter from the bank – that will be the interest rate for our ISAs. Down again. Then I see it. The horrid, familiar, dark envelope, cheap and thin and nasty, with the pale address label stuck on the front.

I lean back against the wall because I simply don't understand. It's over now. Finished. I didn't do anything wrong. Karl and Antony were *not* involved, so nor am I, not really.

My heart pounding, I pause to remind myself of Matthew's instructions. I move into the kitchen and fetch the little box of protective gloves and the evidence bags provided by the police. For a moment I think about popping the envelope inside, unopened, but I find that I can't do that. I have to know why someone would still do this to me. I mean – they must surely have heard on the news. That it wasn't Karl and Antony after all. So why would they still do this? Why?

With the gloves on, I rip it open. Same as before. Can hear my breath now. Find myself looking around the hall, through to the kitchen again. Can just see through to confirm that the bolt is across the back door. Good.

The postcard is black again. Letters cut out from magazines and stuck on. Messy. Not in a straight line.

I AM WATCHING YOU.

I stare at it, reading it over and over as I take out my mobile from my handbag, trying to calm my breathing as I dial Matthew's number.

CHAPTER 44

THE FRIEND

Sarah has been dreading this meeting and sits at the kitchen table, tapping her nails against her mug of coffee.

The past few days – all the long hours with the police – have been utterly exhausting. Caroline, the linchpin of this home, refuge, commune or whatever you want to call it, has been kind and supportive and very obviously a rock for Lily, certainly more helpful than Sarah, who realises only now how desperately she underestimated just how bad going to the police would be.

She had expected swift progress – that the police would arrest her father and get answers about Anna quickly. But they can't seem to find him . . .

She thought, also, that she and Lily would be interviewed together and would be able to support each other, sisters side by side, but she found out too late this is not allowed because of rules to ensure one witness does not lead another. Separate evidence. Separate stories. Separate spells in the special little unit with its soft green sofa and a basket of toys in the corner which haunted Sarah as she realised, with a horrible tingling of her skin, that they were for young children being interviewed about equally horrid things.

The police leading the inquiry into Anna's disappearance were first up. She had to tell them the truth. About the sex on the train and her obsession with Antony. About the row in the club, how she told Anna not to be a baby and pretty much lost track of her from about half past midnight. That Sarah had refused to get the taxi with her when Anna wanted to go back to the hotel. Assumed Anna would be asleep when she got back there herself . . .

Next, the awful truth about her dad. The thing he did when she started her period. The text message the night Anna went missing that she had shown to Anna – asking for them to meet him at the bar of his hotel. The reason Sarah is once more worried he might somehow be involved with Anna.

Then it was poor Lily's turn. Sarah watched her sister being led into the room with the green sofa, while she and Caroline waited outside. Everyone was almost too kind. Just a little bit too fussy. *Tea? Biscuits?* Lots of offers of magazines and more drinks. But it all took ages and ages and ages.

'So, Sarah. Thank you for agreeing to this chat. It's just we need to make some decisions together.' Caroline has her hands cupped around her own mug. The familiar aroma of green tea.

'Have they found my dad?'

Caroline shakes her head. 'At least, they're not telling us if they have.' Sarah cannot stop looking at the bands on Caroline's own wrists. It's not difficult to work out why she runs this place.

'So, the thing is, I've been talking to social services. About going forward now.'

This is unexpected. A sweep of dread through Sarah. Social services? She had no idea this place would liaise with social services. She thought it was independent. The reason it was so off-piste. Own rules. Own oddball way of doing things. No pressure to involve the police unless you want to.

'It's because of your age, Sarah,' Caroline says, as if reading her thoughts. 'And the fact that your mother wants you home. It complicates things.'

'I don't want to see my mother. Can I stay here, *please*? With Lily?'

Caroline nods, and Sarah finds that she is crying with the sudden relief, no longer hearing properly as Caroline goes on to explain about enrolling her in a local sixth form. The various protocols and conditions. That she will sort it all out.

Caroline reaches out to take Sarah's hands and tilts her head. 'Lily still has problems with her anorexia, and I am very concerned about how a trial over your dad – if it gets to that stage – will impact on her. So I need you to cooperate with my house rules if we take this forward. Not talking to people about why we are here – that sort of thing.'

'Will I have to wear the bracelets and have a new name?' Sarah has no idea why she asks this so quickly. It sounds rude and ungrateful. 'Sorry. I didn't mean to say that.'

But Caroline is laughing, which makes Sarah relax even more, the relief now reaching the tips of her fingers. Her toes. Her cheeks flushing.

'You find all that a bit kooky, Sarah?'

'A bit.'

'No pressure, but you might find both help. The bracelets are terrific for easing tension. Something to fiddle with when you feel overwhelmed. I introduced them to help people who self-harm.'

Sarah is suddenly thinking of the marks on her sister's arms before she left home.

'What about the names? Why did you pick Saffron for Lily?'

'Because she came here like someone who wanted to be invisible. To disappear. That's why she stopped eating. And then one day, when I saw her painting, I saw this entirely different person. This vivid energy and colour on the page. Spicy. Evocative. Memorable. "Look at me." And I felt that was who she was meant to be.'

Sarah cannot stop her tears, and Caroline squeezes her hands very gently.

'There is a lot to sort out. Your mother wants contact and we will need to liaise very carefully over that. But if you accept my offer and you wanted a new name' – again Caroline seems to be reading her mind – 'I would suggest Dawn. Just something for you to think about.'

'Why Dawn?'

'Because you don't like yourself very much, Sarah. And no girl of seventeen should hate themselves. Especially when they have experienced what you have. You need a fresh start, lovely. In my opinion, and it is just my opinion, you need the sun to come up.'

CHAPTER 45

THE WITNESS

Trends are such a funny thing. Greenery is back, big time. Suddenly we can't get enough glossy greenery in to bulk out our bouquets and displays. All the restaurants and the brides want it everywhere. Green table runners. Green arches for the doorways. Luscious leaves everywhere. It is a bit like the popularity of baby names. Trends creep up on you. Suddenly everyone is called Amelia. Suddenly everyone wants *greenery.*

I don't mind, actually. Change is good and I enjoy gathering my own greenery from the garden and local lanes. I have always grown lots of hostas for the large leaves and curved shoots, and have found that cuttings from our laurel hedges are working well for larger displays, too. It is good to be doing new things, and to be frank, I need something to distract me. I hate this new limbo. Two weeks since that new postcard and zilch progress. I handed it straight over to Matthew, who passed it on to his friend Melanie Sanders. They ran the usual fingerprint tests, postmark enquiries, blah blah. Nothing. Whoever sends them must wear gloves. Turns out the haters can be clever as well as cruel.

Right now I am making up today's final birthday order while Luke holds the fort front of house. He is looking so much better, and the two contenders interested in his job are calling in to see him later while

I'm in Cornwall with Matthew. He'll vet them first. I'll only see them if they are OK about the hours. I've had a couple of time-wasters over the ad in the window, horrified at the very early starts. I guess teenagers like their weekend lie-ins.

I set everything out as usual – ribbons, tape, pins – and begin the bouquet. A combination of roses and stocks, in pink and purple, with some rosemary for the scent. I do my usual trick of twisting and building slowly to keep the balance and the rhythm. It is a fortieth birthday bouquet, and so I add in a couple more flowers than usual as I remember my fortieth so well. I check the display, bind it, trim the ends and then pop it into a vase just to circle it, walking round to check from all angles before wrapping it in tissue and ribbon.

I pop it into the cooler and move through to Luke to remind him that it is not for delivery, that the husband is calling in for it later. It's prepaid, all written up in the book.

And then I check my watch and Luke is telling me not to worry about the shop, that he has it all in hand, and reminds me he is seeing his potential replacements later. Girl first, then boy. They both did the Ten Tors same time as him apparently, so are solid. Used to early starts. Reliable. If they both seem sane, he will leave their CVs and contact details on the shelf under the counter and I can decide whether to see them myself or to advertise. He would like to stop working by Christmas at the very latest so that he can concentrate on his studies. *Is that OK?*

I smile. I like that Luke is doing this for me; that he is sleeping better and doing OK back at school. It's been a tough time.

And then the text comes. Matthew is waiting in his car outside. I don't want Luke worrying; I tell him I am off to see a potential client in Cornwall and will be back late afternoon. I kiss Luke on the forehead and he pulls a face, so I wink my goodbye and remind him to text if there are any worries. I warn him that Cornwall can be a bit patchy for signal, so not to panic if I don't reply immediately.

Climbing into Matthew's car, I smile at the evidence of his very different new life. Dark circles still under his eyes – the parental clutter of a nursery rhymes CD, spare bibs, a pink blanket in the back. A soft yellow duck on the parcel shelf. The 'Baby on Board' sticker, which Matthew tells me his wife insisted upon.

'You sure you're feeling OK about this, Ella?' Matthew looks over his shoulder as he reverses out of the parking space. I think of the headlights that so frightened me those early mornings in the past. This was the exact parking spot. It was probably someone in the flats above the shops. I put on my seatbelt and try not to dwell on it. *Enough now, Ella.*

'A bit nervous, but I want to come.'

I didn't honestly know what to think when Matthew first rang me. It was a shock. Mrs Ballard getting in touch with him. At first I wondered if it was to be some kind of formal complaint – me sending him down there that time. Suspecting her of sending the postcards. But no. Something even more surprising.

It is starting to rain and Matthew apologises. His windscreen wipers make an annoying squeaking noise. He tells me that replacing the blades is on a long list of things he may not get around to until his daughter goes to university. I laugh. He laughs.

'It gets easier,' I say. 'Once they sleep.'

'Oh, I'm not complaining,' he says, and he is wearing that open expression I so like. Relaxed. Straight. Kind. I find myself looking at his profile and wondering again why he left the force. He avoids the question very cleverly whenever I raise it.

We make good time, stopping only to buy takeaway coffees. We listen to the radio mostly, and only once we are within ten minutes does he talk through his own strategy. Clever of him not to wind me up earlier.

The latest from the Met police is not good news. They have just discounted Sarah's father from the inquiry into Anna's disappearance. He was found in Norwich somewhere. I don't know the details, in fact I'm not supposed to know this at all, but off the record Matthew says that CCTV from the hotel where he was staying the night Anna went missing, along with mobile phone tracking, has provided a cast-iron alibi. He was in his hotel room when Anna went missing. No question. Cameras in the hallway show he only emerged when Sarah's mum phoned him.

Mrs Ballard is now desperate. She wants to employ Matthew herself to review Anna's disappearance: to try to see if the police have missed anything. She believes the case has gone completely 'cold'. With no suspects left, the investigating team is being quietly reduced in number. Matthew, equally surprised by her sudden approach, says he has made it very clear that he is highly unlikely to be able to make progress alone. But he feels compassion for the family and wants to at least hear Mrs Ballard out. However, having been engaged by me first over the postcards, there is a potential conflict of interest and that's why he has asked me along.

'I remain almost certain that Mrs Ballard isn't behind the cards, but I need to see you in the same room to make this call. I hate to be so blunt and to use you like a guinea pig but that's where we are, Ella.' He has said this already to me on the phone, and I do understand.

'I can't just work for you both. But I do worry about whether this Anna case will ever be solved now. It's very sad for the family. Very tough.' He is glancing at me. 'But it's upsetting for you too, Ella. My first call is your feelings.'

'I know that. And I don't think I'll ever be happy until they find out what happened to her.' I pause. 'Do you think there's any chance at all she's still alive, Matthew?'

'Very little. But Mrs Ballard won't want to hear that. The mothers never do.' Again he glances at me and then at the baby clutter. 'I'm only coming to completely understand that now.'

We drive in silence for a time and I glance at him once, twice, finding myself frowning. 'Do you mind me asking again, Matthew. Why you left the force?' It seems such a shame to me; he seems so very good at this. So decent . . .

He keeps his eyes fixed firmly on the road ahead as we see a signpost for the farm, a right turning ahead.

'Guilt.' He says the word quietly, turning to me as I narrow my eyes. 'There was a case. A child died. It wasn't my fault, technically. But . . .'

I see his eyes change and wish I had not pushed him. I fidget with the seatbelt as he clears his throat and indicates to take the turning. I understand now.

'OK. Here we are, then. You ready for this, Ella?'

I nod, and my stomach grips as we take the strange, narrow approach road to the farmhouse. I am thinking of that awful time I came down here myself. The tussle on the doorstep. The other reason Matthew says he needs assurance that Mrs Ballard has finally made peace over my own place in this.

As she opens the door, Mrs Ballard's face is strained, her tone all effort. She looks older and thinner and I feel so sorry for her. 'I can't thank you enough for coming. Both of you.' At first she cannot quite look at me. Not yet. And I see Matthew taking this in.

She fusses over making coffee, and though neither of us needs a drink, we accept her clattering about as an icebreaker. Something to ease things.

I admire the kitchen. The house. The large Aga. And then I feel embarrassed at my small talk, noting the pictures on the fridge. Anna as a little girl, unmistakable with her striking blonde hair. In most of the snaps she is with an older girl. Her sister, I assume. A few other photos with friends. A shot in a paddling pool. Anna doing cartwheels on the lawn.

Matthew kicks off the 'business' discussion. He asks Mrs Ballard outright if she understands that he remains engaged by me to investigate the postcards. Is she comfortable with this?

'I understand from Ella that you visited her shop in the past? And that you were very upset when she called here once before.'

'That was my fault,' I say quickly.

'No.' Mrs Ballard leads the way through to the sitting room with her tray. It is a gorgeous room with French doors onto the garden. In the corner, a beautiful grand piano.

'I was not myself, Ella. I apologise. I can understand why you might have thought it was me who sent the postcards, but I promise you I didn't. I came to the shop because at that time I did blame you. It wasn't fair, but I just didn't know where to put my anger.'

'I do understand.'

Matthew talks for quite a while about the difficulties of these kinds of investigations. He talks about his contact in the force, about the frustration at the dead ends. The confirmation that Sarah's father, who remains in custody 'on other matters', has a cast-iron alibi for the night Anna went missing. Mrs Ballard says she's heard the same via Sarah.

'So, no suspects left.' Mrs Ballard puts down her mug. 'Which is why I need your help, Matthew. I have some savings.' The desperation in her voice is dreadful, and I watch her eyes as Matthew says he will need to think about things and get back to her.

There is this terrible impasse, and so I admire the piano, mention that I had lessons until my teens and regret giving it up. I move over to examine it close up and to take in the beautifully framed photographs along the top. Anna with her sister again, as bridesmaids. Family groups.

And then, such a shock. An extraordinary punch to my gut. The disorientation so great that I feel unsteady.

'Who's this?' I pick up the photograph and turn to Matthew and Barbara Ballard, an image from the past forming again in my head. Not understanding this . . .

'That's the girls with a friend. When they did the Ten Tors.' Mrs Ballard's tone is wary.

'But he was *on the train*.'

'I'm sorry?'

'This boy – the boy with the curly hair. He was on the train to London that day. When Anna went to London.'

'I'm sorry but you must be mistaken. No . . . no. That's not possible. He was away.'

'I'm telling you it was him.' I am looking at the photograph again and then at Matthew, who has stood up and is walking across to me. 'It was definitely him, Matthew. I nearly spilled my coffee on him . . .'

It was after that awful scene, when I passed the toilet. *Sarah, oh Sarah* . . . When I decided to move seats to the other end of the train. We were going around a bend. I lost my balance, walking through the aisle.

I'm sorry. The lid loose on my coffee.

It's OK. Don't worry. It's fine.

He looked right at me. Definitely him . . . That hair. Those eyes.

'Who is this, Mrs Ballard?' Matthew has taken the photograph from me and is holding it out to her, trying to make her look.

CHAPTER 46

ANNA

July 2015

She is shocked and shaken but also angry with Sarah. She marches after her to try again, pushing through the people all crowded together, dancing and drinking. Suddenly the club is too dark. Too noisy. Too alien. The smell of sweat and alcohol everywhere she turns. She feels a little giddy.

'We promised to stick *together*.' She grabs at Sarah's arm but can hear that her own words are slurring slightly – sees now that Sarah is unsteady, too. 'We really need to go now. I don't feel safe. Please, Sarah. I'm begging you . . .'

'Oh, for goodness sake, don't be such a baby, Anna. So dramatic.' Sarah again shakes her off. 'I told you already. If you want to go, just go. But I'm not ready. Why don't you just lighten up. Have another drink.'

'I've had enough here, Sarah. We need to go.'

'Then – you go. I'll see you later. Back at the hotel.' And then Sarah is gone again, through the crowd, heading after Antony into one of the other rooms.

Anna stands very still, just watching her. She has to position her legs wider apart to stop the swaying. Everything is swaying. The room and the shadows and the lights and the people. The music pounding right through the floor and up through her body. She feels her eyes narrowing and her vision is ever so slightly blurred. She sees a man looking at her, swigging from his beer bottle. He winks. She looks away, suddenly all paranoia. Again checks her handbag, its long strap across her body. Checks the zip. Her purse. Her phone.

She follows the signs to the toilets and waits for a free cubicle. Puts down the lid. Sits down and leans forward to try to calm herself; takes out her phone. She skims the contacts. *Home.* She looks at the word, blurring in front of her. She thinks of her dad in the car. How angry with him she was. The photograph. Him and *that woman.* She lets her finger hover for a moment but then – no. She wipes her thumb against her dress. She considers the fallout; that her mother will never, ever let her do anything on her own again. She sits for a while, wonders how long it will be until she feels more steady. For just a moment, she thinks of Sarah's dad but then remembers the warning . . . *If you phone my dad, I will never speak to you again.*

Anna has had too much to drink before, but never on her own. Not like this. She wishes that she had downloaded the app for taxis but Sarah had said she would do that.

She has no choice, then. Anna decides to go outside and hail a cab. She remembers that it must be a black cab, has read about the danger of fake minicab drivers. She feels afraid and so, to calm herself, she tries to picture herself in the back of the cab. Safe. Right up to the front door of the hotel. Where she will ring Sarah and maybe her parents next, even the police if Sarah *still* won't listen, still won't come . . .

Outside it is drizzling. There are a few people smoking. Quite a narrow street. Hardly any traffic. She waits a while and tries not to look at anyone. But no cars pass. No taxis. She sees the bouncer at the door and wonders if he might help her find a cab but he is suddenly distracted by a group of three men who are playing up because he won't let them in.

She is getting wet. Still feels so unsteady on her feet. And then . . .

'Anna. What on *earth* are you doing here?'

She turns, and relief and surprise and a whole myriad of emotions flood through her so that she bursts into tears.

'Tim. Oh my God.'

He is shushing her and she is embarrassed and relieved all at once. Wiping her face with her sleeve.

'Oh God, Tim, I'm so pleased to see you. But what on earth . . . I thought you were in Scotland?' She is clutching at both his arms, using them to steady herself. Confusion. Relief. Disorientation.

'Where's Sarah?' Tim is looking right into her face.

'In the club. She won't come. I'm trying to find a taxi. I can't make her come.'

'Well, you won't find a cab here. No chance.' He is glancing around the street. 'Come on. This way. Let's get you out of this rain.'

Tim is leading her then by the arm, and she expects him to take her into a doorway. A café or a pub or something. The tube? But he is saying that the tube stopped hours ago and they need to get to a place where they can order her a cab. 'This way. We need to take the night bus. Just a few stops. Then we can get you a taxi easily.'

They seem to be walking quite a long way. A bus stop. Then on the bus. No one else. She asks, 'Does the bus go near the hotel?' She gives him the address again. He says no. It doesn't go that far. But she is not to worry. They will be able to order her a cab for the last stretch.

And then they are off the bus, walking again. And Tim is saying, 'Here it is. The flat. Here. We can get you dry and order the cab from here. Wait in the dry.' She can hear keys jangling. There is a porch which is keeping them dry. And then they are inside.

A narrow hall, then a sitting room with a bay window. Brown curtains.

He is explaining that this is the flat left to him by his father. To be rented out so the income can fund him through uni. That was the deal in the will. The reason he is in town. The trip to Scotland got cancelled. This flat is normally let. 'Remember, I told you all, when my dad died?'

She does, sort of. Vaguely. Tim's dad showed no interest in him all his life, then suddenly got cancer. Got God. Got in touch. No one else in his life, so put Tim in his will . . . She is glad to be safe. Out of the rain. But where is the tenant? And how far are they from her hotel now?

Tim says the tenant has just done a bunk and he's in town to tidy the place up. Sort out a new lease. He was planning to contact her tomorrow to explain Scotland was cut short; see if he could meet her and Sarah after all.

'I thought you girls were at a musical tonight?'

She explains how the club was recommended online. Does not mention Karl and Antony. Ashamed. She can hear her words slurring still and tries to speak more slowly. She feels so embarrassed; she does not want Tim to judge her. She is trying to sound sensible, but she is wondering now what he was doing near the club. He says he had a curry with a mate at an Indian nearby.

'Just as well, eh? You shouldn't be on your own, Anna. Not in London. Especially that bit. Dodgy area.'

'You were there.'

'It's different for blokes.'

And now Anna needs to sit down. She's still so woozy.

'Right. We need to make sure Sarah is OK, too,' he is saying. 'I'll go back for her once you're OK. She'll be safe in the club for now.' He is taking out his phone; she hears him ordering a cab for her. Double-checks the name of her hotel. He says cabs are more reliable this time of night when you order them to come to an address. They are saying it will be fifteen minutes. Not too bad. Right. So he will see her off safely, then he will go back himself for Sarah. Bring her to the hotel. Is she OK with this?

Anna is thinking that maybe they should have gone back in for Sarah straight away. She is grateful but confused, and begins to cry again. He is sitting next to her, his arm around her shoulders. Tells her not to worry. That it is *all right now, Anna.* He is going to make sure that everything is all right.

And then she closes her eyes. And she is remembering the awful picture Tim sent her this morning. Her dad with April – Tim's mum. She hasn't wanted to mention it, to think about it even, but wonders why he hasn't said anything either.

'Why did you send me the picture, Tim?' She is still crying. 'I mean – why this morning?'

It hit her phone just before her dad drove her to the station. Such a terrible shock.

You disgust me.

'I just felt you had the right to know. It was a terrible shock to me, too. I thought we should decide together what to do. Whether to tell your mum.'

'I wish you hadn't. I had a big row with my dad.'

'Sorry. I didn't think.'

'But how did you get it? The photo?' It was so graphic. So foul. Her dad and April. Naked. Her legs up in the air on the bed. Like porn. Disgusting . . .

And now Tim is standing, saying he doesn't want to talk about that anymore just now, and that he will make them coffee. It will do her good. She is thinking that there isn't time, surely. No point. With the taxi? But he says even a few sips will do her good. 'The state you're in . . .'

While he is gone, cluttering about in another room, Anna begins to glance around. And now she doesn't understand. There are quite a few books on one of the shelves. Walking books and map books. And there are magazines, too, ones she knows that Tim likes. She narrows her eyes. There's a stack – months' worth of them. She looks down at the coffee table: they're from the past three months. It doesn't make sense.

'You OK in there, Anna?'

'Fine.'

She reaches down to the shelf under the coffee table to find a book of walks in Cornwall. A frisson of unease passes through her. The book has several places marked with bookmarks. No. Not bookmarks. She flicks the pages to find that there are photographs marking the chapters.

The first makes her smile. It is a group shot – that birthday party her mum threw for Tim. They are wearing hats made from balloons, and she and Sarah are clutching sausage dogs that the boys made. Tim and Paul.

She turns the pages to the next photograph, and then suddenly there is this truly odd feeling within her. Like a change of temperature. For it is a picture of her, taken from a distance. She is at her bedroom window looking out, just about to draw the curtains.

Anna can feel her heart rate increasing. Her muscles tensing. She flicks through the book to find more pictures – just of her. Her playing on the lawn. Her sitting in a tree. All of them taken from a distance.

She puts the book back and stands just as Tim returns with two mugs.

'How long till the taxi, Tim?'

'Not long now.'

'I think I need the loo.' She tries to hide that her hands are shaking by her sides.

'Sit down. You'll be back at the hotel in a moment. You can go there.' There is a change in his tone. Clipped. Not nice. Not Tim. He is standing between her and the door.

She looks at him, the temperature even colder inside her.

'The bathroom here isn't nice, Anna.'

'Oh, right.'

'Drink your coffee. Just remember it's a good job I found you.' Finally, he sits and sips his drink. 'A very good job I watch out for you, Anna. That I always watch out for you.'

'Yes. Very true. I'm grateful, Tim.' She is looking at the magazines and the book of walks, her heart thump-thump-thumping in her chest.

'Did you say the tenant did a bunk?'

'Yeah. Last week. We need to find another tenant.' He has started to rock in his seat. To and fro . . .

She can feel her shoulders starting to tremble and is worried he will see this. She looks at the books on the shelves. Notices that some of them are A-level books. Tim's A-level subjects.

'Let's wait in the doorway. Look out for the cab, shall we?' She has stood up again.

'No. Sit down. Drink your coffee.' That clipped tone again. He twitches his head. Rocks faster.

'I think I need the air, Tim.'

'You're fine, Anna. You're with me now. You're fine when you're with me.'

She sips her drink. She can hear her breath. Her pulse. Her heart. She can feel the dread building and building, the temperature falling and falling – but knows, too, even through the booze and the fear, that she must not let him see this. Little black dots on the edge of this scene, closing in. Not real.

'Could I have some water, Tim?'

'No. You're fine.' Tim has started to rock faster. To. Fro. To. Fro. He is all agitation suddenly. Strange, jerky movements of his head.

'It's OK. I'll get the water.' She stands and moves towards the door to the hall, slowly at first, but then faster and suddenly he is grabbing at her from behind. Instinctively she kicks back hard with her right leg and he recoils for a moment.

She makes it through to the hall, just feet from the door, but feels a blow suddenly to the back of her head. Blackness for a moment. Then